THE RING

THE RING

ELISABETH HOREM

Translated by Jane Kuntz

DALKEY ARCHIVE PRESS
CHAMPAIGN / LONDON / DUBLIN

Originally published in 1994 as *Le Ring* by Bernard Campiche Editeur, Orbe, Switzerland

First Edition, 2013

Library of Congress Cataloging-in-Publication Data
is available.
ISBN: 978-1-56478-868-9

Partially funded by a grant from the Illinois Arts Council, a state agency

The publication of this work was supported by grants from the Swiss Arts Council Pro Helvetia and the Office de la culture du canton de Berne/SWISSLOS.

swiss arts council
prohelvetia

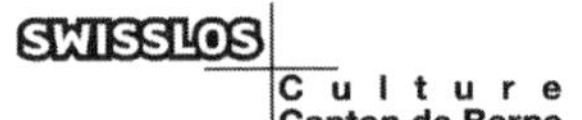

www.dalkeyarchive.com

Cover: design and composition by Mikhail Iliatov

Printed on permanent/durable acid-free paper

PART ONE

It took only a few minutes for Louise to break the news, not the news he'd wanted to hear.

It came as a complete surprise. And to top it off, Gilles had been hired by an American university.

America, no less.

It looked sunny and warm through the bare window. Louise removed her scarf. Around her neck, she was wearing a small diamond pendant that he recognized immediately. His head throbbed with mute anger.

"What are you smiling about?"

Had he smiled, really? He certainly hadn't felt like smiling, but since she said he had, fine.

Emboldened by the smile, then, he replied casually:

"Funny that you should be leaving, because it just so happens I'm leaving too. I was actually about to tell you."

Touché. She raised a skeptical brow, waiting for more. As he was not forthcoming, she asked, "Where to?" with a caustic little laugh.

At first he was tempted to say it was none of her business anymore, but that would have risked sounding brutal, losing him his momentary advantage. So he improvised.

"Tahas."

He could no longer recall how Gilles and she had met. They had got along from the start. She chided him for being cold toward his brother; she wanted him to ask Gilles out more. One day, he chanced to see them together in a restaurant. They couldn't see him from where they were sitting, but he had a good view of them thanks to a reflection. They looked like anything but a couple in love. It seemed more like a business lunch. She never said a word about the meeting, nor did he ever bring it up.

Now, there they were, arm in arm, setting off for a new life, one he had trouble imagining. They would be crossing an ocean, leaving him alone on the nether shore. He couldn't bear the idea, so he had tossed out a city name at random, in order not to be the one left behind.

Again, that old trap of unrequited love.

While waiting for Louise in that café in the old town, Quentin had read the newspaper. He skimmed the headlines distractedly, occasionally glancing out the window. As there was still no sign of Louise, he began looking through the classifieds. One sought a man in his thirties or forties, preferably unmarried, with a college degree (major unspecified). He needed to be flexible and to enjoy travel. Applications were to be sent to Tahas—a city whose very name sounded exotic.

So, sitting there with Louise now, feeling desperate, eye riveted on the pendant that Gilles had dared remove from their mother's jewelry box, the name of Tahas sprang naturally to mind.

The afternoon was endless, his coworkers tiresome. The telephone's ring jangled his nerves. Even the April sun that he, like everyone else, had found so delightful now annoyed him. Pretending to have a toothache, he went home.

He devoured a whole bar of chocolate (which he immediately regretted) and wondered whether he wouldn't have been better off back at work.

Not a day went by that he didn't relive the terrible, haunting image of a body lying on the sidewalk, covered by a pink raincoat.

He had just turned seven. His mother had sent him to buy some milk. "Careful not to break it," she had warned, as he set off proudly clutching a large coin in one hand and in the other a net shopping bag with an empty bottle. The store wasn't far, but with two streets to cross, it was something of an adventure.

He took tiny steps all the way back for fear of dropping the bottle. Thirty years on, he could still feel the cold contact of glass on his bare legs through the netting.

Outside their building, a crowd was gathering around something he couldn't see. Police were on the scene. He drew closer to have a look, curious but intimidated. He heard someone say, "Oh my God, there's her kid!" and people began to move away from him, as if terrified.

A woman lay beneath a bright raincoat, a pink color he liked very much, one that little boys were unfortunately never allowed to wear.

His mother had just jumped from the sixth floor. What followed was a muddle in his memory. He must have fallen, for the bottle had broken. A neighbor took him to her place, gave him clean socks, as his were sopping wet with milk, and dabbed his knee with some Mercurochrome. Later, Aunt Cathy would come get him. Gilles was at boarding school, and was spared the sight of their mother laid out under the raincoat. She was wearing the little diamond-studded cloverleaf necklace, that day.

Nothing so ephemeral as news. Take the dailies, for instance: yesterday's, so avidly sought twenty-four hours ago, are of no interest to anyone today. The new, freshly inked paper makes yesterday's useless, relegating it to the status of dead pulp, something to wrap your potatoes with, or to line the trash bin.

Quentin had a terrible time obtaining the two-day-old newspaper. To find it, he had to sort through a pile of papers a neighbor had nicely bound and set next to the garbage.

He found the ad he was after, tore it out, and stuffed it in his pocket.

He was somewhat taken aback by the answer he got: a certain Mr. Moser wrote him from Tahas to say that his application had been favorably reviewed and that he himself, director of the Parker Company, would be pleased to welcome him to the staff as of June first.

This all seemed disconcertingly simple. Not a word about what the company actually did. Nor the slightest hint as to what might be expected of him at the workplace. The letter did mention—and this was the only concrete item—that he would need to purchase his own plane ticket, reimbursable upon his signing the contract. Finally, he was asked to kindly confirm his arrival at the earliest convenience.

He had to admit this all sounded like some kind of joke. A joke of his own making, after all. The whole idea of leaving for Tahas had been a complete coincidence, an elaborate lie he had let play out a bit longer by answering the ad. He had never really intended to up and quit his job, to leave the country simply because his lover was marrying his brother. More power to them. The letter from this Moser fellow had brought the whole matter to a close. He should throw it out, and with it the memory of the entire episode.

But what had begun as a hoax had assumed more substance with each passing day, and as he waited for news from Tahas, he had begun to take it seriously.

He reread the letter.

The company stationery reassured him somewhat. Mention of a telex number seemed an encouraging sign. The absence of any solid information was perhaps motivated by a concern for discretion.

He tried to imagine himself in charge—of what?—of some secret mission? It simply didn't add up, though he was looking at the letter now with increased interest.

He left it on the corner of his desk.

Every so often, the luminous spiderweb of a city would drift slowly beneath the belly of the aircraft, then vanish. Inexplicable glittering paths cut across the blackness below and ended mysteriously like threads of gossamer suddenly broken up by great interstellar winds.

Then the plane began its descent toward Tahas, dipping one wing, then the other, slowly decelerating, as if some invisible celestial moorings were holding it back. A constant stream of shapes was slipping beneath the wing now, circles, triangles, stars, and Quentin thought to himself that men had labored to design these figures and that the resulting work, the fruit of their daily toil, had surpassed their intentions, without their ever knowing, to join the concert of heavenly bodies. Out of this luminous mosaic emerged an altogether different humanity, more beautiful, more united, disembodied, awe-inspiring. He closed his eyes until the moment he felt the plane meet the hard grain of the tarmac. The spell was broken. Only the little bluish landing lights, phosphorescent forget-me-nots, still formed straight lines that ran to the horizon and beyond. What came next was pure chaos: the piles of luggage, the throng, the cacophony of loudspeakers, people staggering pathetically under the weight of their bags, constantly having to move aside to avoid obstacles, like disoriented ants. Nothing remained of that harmonious world glimpsed only moments before, a world where the same wind blew across the Milky Way and the cities of humanity.

For the first night, they put him up in the Grand Hotel. His room looked out onto a pleasant corner of lawn, but since he was only on the second floor, he didn't have what could be called "a view." He felt a twinge of disappointment, for he had imagined himself on that first night in Tahas sitting on the balcony outside his room, a glass of whiskey in hand, ice cubes tinkling as they melted, staring out at the lights on the opposite shore as they plunged their reflections into the dark water like festooned banderillas.

But that's not how it went at all, since his room had no balcony looking onto the Ovir; nor did he really feel like whiskey, a drink he didn't particularly care for. He was feeling sleepy more than anything else.

An English-language newspaper had been left on his table. He scanned the headlines and nearly dozed off. He'd be better off just turning in for the night, since the time change meant he would be losing three hours of sleep, and he was supposed to report to the Parker Company early the next morning.

The building where the company had its offices was easy to spot: no other façade on the Ring—or in the entire city, for that matter—was painted in such bright candy colors: plum purple, strawberry red, pistachio green. The lobby walls were covered almost entirely in marble, engraved with all kinds of inscriptions followed by floor numbers, calling to mind certain chapels lined with ex-votos. Or a columbarium.

The secretary who greeted Quentin seemed unaware of his existence. She asked him to wait a moment, then disappeared behind a door. Right next to the entrance, a man sat reading a newspaper. A tabloid, surmised Quentin, based on the headlines. A gemstone ring attracted attention to the man's thick, hairy fingers. Nothing in this person's outward attitude suggested that he had noticed Quentin's presence.

A glass case displayed a collection of objects: a model tractor, some dolls in traditional dress, embroidered place mats in a grayish color, and two plates decorated with hand-painted flowers—in all likelihood, samples of local crafts. It all looked rather dusty. On top of the case sat a trophy, a winner's cup for some soccer match.

Quentin nearly jumped when the door opened. It was only a woman bringing a cup of coffee. She had an unpleasant face, pallid, round, and flat as a moon. She passed by without paying him the slightest attention and set the cup on the desk of the man who grunted something from behind his newspaper.

The secretary had been gone for a while now, and Quentin was starting to wonder whether there had been a misunderstanding. He sought comfort in the fact that they had reserved him a room in the Grand Hotel, a room whose luxury had even flattered him a bit, and that this was the clearest proof that they were indeed expecting him.

The woman finally returned, then proceeded to walk him along a corridor cluttered with boxes and files piled right on the floor, leading him into a tiny office whose size struck him as odd, since he'd had time to read "Conference Room" on the door.

The man receiving him looked tired, even sick. He was having trouble completing his sentences, and several times passed a hand over his eyes, like someone who hadn't slept much, who couldn't stand the light. He first asked Quentin how he was doing, whether he'd had a good trip, whether the hotel room was suitable.

He spoke haltingly, as though struggling to gather his thoughts. Quentin's being hired by the Parker Company seemed of no interest to him whatsoever. There was a silence. He leaned on his elbows, thrust his torso forward, and began diligently joining his fingers, two by two, thumb to thumb, index to index, and so on. When the ring fingers had come together, he resumed:

"Unfortunately, the director is away today. He's on a trip in the south of the country for a few days. He asked me to tell you how sorry he is not to be here to welcome you. But since his departure was rather last-minute, he didn't have time to let me know exactly what your job here will be all about. It's unfortunate, I know. Well, at any rate, if I understood correctly, it wasn't so much for a specific job that Mr. Moser has brought you on board—we already have perfectly qualified employees, you understand, all quite competent—as to . . . well, to back him up, to help him out more generally, and to, uh . . . bolster the . . . what's the word? . . . the uh, European staff, yes that's it, the European staff of our company."

He rubbed his eyes once again, breathing a little sigh of relief as though, as far as he was concerned, the hardest part was over.

"Madame Farge will show you your office. Feel free to ask her any questions you might have about settling in. You can also talk to Mr. Masko, our local assistant for . . . well, for all sorts of issues."

In a supreme effort, he rose from his chair and shook Quentin's hand. It was only at this point that Quentin noticed he reeked of alcohol.

The secretary walked him to an office that was nicely furnished but had no window, which confirmed the unpleasant overall impression he was getting from the place. An engraving above his desk depicted a sunset over a lake. On closer inspection, what he at first took to be rocks were in fact crocodiles lazing near the water, which he imagined as murky and disease infested. Behind him, something rolled, then fell with a sharp click: it was a clock that counted out little steel marbles at the rate of one per minute.

Everything was settled very quickly. Moser's assistant (whose name he never did find out) accepted Quentin's resignation without making any trouble. He seemed distracted, not really listening. He was apparently indifferent to whether or not the staff was European, and seemed little concerned by what his superior might think of the matter.

When Quentin shut the door for the last time on the crocodiles and the clock, he sensed he'd somehow made a narrow escape. The only person he'd taken to at all was Masko, so he dropped by his office to say good-bye.

Everything Masko told him about the Parker Company and the two men who ran it confirmed his conviction that he had done well to quit.

"Yes, you're definitely doing the right thing," Masko told him. "And anyway, you probably have other plans in Tahas, don't you?"

This simple question caught Quentin off guard, for he had no plans of any kind. He had toyed with the idea of going back to Europe, but he basically felt no real desire to do so. So Masko suggested he drop by the Consulate: he had heard they were looking for an emergency replacement for someone in the visa section.

"They'll surely be delighted to add a European to their local staff," he added bemusedly.

There was a short silence. A flash of something else in Masko's look that Quentin was having trouble identifying. They parted on a chillier than expected note.

The Grand Hotel was not too far and he had seen no need

to take a taxi, but it was so hot out that he soon wished he had. Halfway there, he suddenly felt terribly weary. The traffic noise on the Ring was deafening. He had forgotten his sunglasses, and felt as if the sun were boring into his skull. The hotel seemed to be receding into the distance, like a mirage. He made it at last, relieved at the idea that he would finally be able to lie down. He had a splitting headache.

In the elevator, what he had sought in vain to identify a short while ago finally became obvious: it was contempt.

"Looks like we've got ourselves another oddball," quipped Rosemonde Goult. "Seems he was supposed to work for some company or other here, but he quit the job on day one. Strange, since he came all the way to Tahas just for the job; that's what I heard, anyway. Something must have happened to make him bail on the very first day. In any case, he must not be a very stable person. I wouldn't be surprised if he quit this job too. Thirty-seven, I saw on his passport: not an age when you should be switching jobs so often. Quentin Corval, funny name. Never met a Quentin before, unless you count the city of Saint-Quentin. Kind of a nice name, actually. I'll have to write my niece who's having a baby. She doesn't know what to call it. Agnes! Did you steal my stapler again? They told her it was a boy, but they're not always right. I'm actually not so sure I would have wanted them to tell me, you're having a girl, or you're having a boy. Not that it's any better when women say 'I'm having Caroline,' or 'I'm having Claude-Henri.' Idiotic. Anyway, it's due next month, right in the middle of summer, poor girl. At least it won't be as hot there as it is here—though there are summers when it does get awfully hot there too. Claudine, are you the one who keeps turning off the air conditioning? Switch it back on, we can't breathe in here. I don't know what's wrong with me today, I guess I'm a little under the weather. Must have been something I ate. I should have passed on those shrimp last night, in this heat . . ."

This is how Paul Gaudin heard of Quentin for the first time. He thought to himself that this Quentin would need help finding someplace to live. And that something had to be done to soundproof these offices. He then mused that he had never been to any city called Saint-Quentin, or if he had, it was a long while ago, yes, maybe before he had met Jeanne in any case, and he had forgotten.

Quentin Corval. The name itself conjured up a medieval castle in black stone, somewhere in Ireland or Scotland, in an untamed landscape of gray rock and peat bogs. (A cold, spume-laden wind whistling across the weathered vegetation.) But the report open on his desk prevented him from pursuing this vision any further, and he stopped thinking about Quentin Corval altogether.

A few weeks after his arrival, Quentin still knew very little of Tahas. Force of habit had already blunted his earlier curiosity, and he sensed he most likely wouldn't be learning much more about the place.

The city was enormous. When seen from the panoramic restaurant, The Himalaya, it stretched as far as the eye could see. The horizon was always drowned in a variably thick layer of smog depending on how strong the winds were, and there were days when he could hardly make out the Grand Hotel from his place, a mere three hundred meters away. Beneath this haze, the city appeared without structure or boundary, like a human swamp. What was called "downtown"—actually, just a neighborhood like many others—was located inside the Ring, that wide boulevard which described a perfect circle on the city map. Twenty years ago, all foreign residents in Tahas were obliged to live on the Ring and nowhere else. With the new regime, that rule was relaxed, along with many others, but the curious custom remained, and foreigners went on living there, even now, with a few rare exceptions. What had been established as a constraint, and felt like one by those it affected, gradually turned out to be more convenient than they had thought. It in no way impeded their ability to get around; on the contrary, it spared them getting caught in traffic jams. What's more, the Ring had the rather peculiar feature of being raised several meters above ground level, like a big circular slide. The buildings that lined it had their entrance at street level, but what looked like the ground floor was in fact one story up. The illusion was further reinforced by the presence of meager gardens out front. On closer inspection, what looked like little gardens were in fact hedges of potted shrubs lined up behind the iron grills.

This distribution of the foreign colony along the same boulevard was particularly advantageous for diplomats in that it simplified their contacts. In any other capital, managing in one evening to attend a holiday gathering, one or two cocktail parties, and then a dinner, would be inconceivable. In Tahas, it was perfectly feasible. Since all the homes holding the events were located on the Ring, one had only to make a succession of stops at the appointed places. The return trip consisted quite naturally of coming full circle, arriving conveniently back home without having to wander through unfamiliar neighborhoods, attempting to decipher dimly lit street names written in foreign lettering, losing one's way under the combined effects of fatigue, disorientation, and alcohol.

But Quentin was not a diplomat, thank God, and his utterly subaltern position at the consulate spared him the need to make the nightly thirteen-kilometer circuit. He preferred to stay at home most evenings, reading or watching local television shows of which he understood not a word, but which relaxed him for that very reason.

He liked his new apartment. He had almost settled in, though he lacked the will to address certain details and be done with them. The apartment already suited him just as it was, and he knew very well that the last things which remained to be done—hanging a few pictures, having some curtains made, or changing the glass tabletop he had broken the first day by setting a hot pan on it—would never get done. Louise used to enjoy making all-day projects out of rearranging something that was perfectly fine to start with, or fixing things that weren't broken. She was one of those people who got passionate about having faucets changed or heaters serviced. If she had been there, she would have taken charge, not resting until she had hung the engravings, ordered the curtains, and had the glass tabletop replaced. Not doing any of this felt a little like revenge, which he found gratifying.

It all worked out well in the end. At the consulate, he was off by two and had his afternoons free. In the morning, he began much earlier than he had at his previous job, but since his colleagues had no qualms about arriving late and leaving on time, it wasn't long before he was doing the same.

When he first arrived, the wing where he was supposed to work was under repair, so they put him temporarily in a little prefab annex located behind the main building, back in a kind of garden.

There was a restroom and sink, a refrigerator, and an electric kettle and cups for making coffee, allowing him to stay holed up in his little hideout all day. Hardly anyone ever came out to bother him, and soon they simply forgot he was there. The time came when he was dealing with no one but the office boy, who brought him papers from time to time, or a new ration of passports to be stamped.

From the start, he kept his distance from the redhead who was handling his own paperwork, the one he'd given his passport to on the first day. The milky flab of her fat arms aroused in him both disgust and fascination, as did her name, which he found a bit sickening to pronounce. Rosemonde Goult talked incessantly, broadcasting a misfortune, predicting a fall from grace, tracking a marriage on the rocks. She was the herald of love affairs and secret flaws, the standard-bearer of rumor. The three other secretaries, markedly younger than she, were much less talkative. Since they all wore their hair more or less the same, it took Quentin a while to tell them apart. For the first few days, they assumed the aspect of a three-headed feminine being, pleasant enough to look at, but without leaving any particular impression on him. It was only gradually that the tricephalous creature broke into three persons who, apart from frequenting the same hair salon, were quite distinct from each other. While he was still living at the Hotel de l'Étoile (far less sumptuous than the Grand Hotel, where he'd ended up having to foot the bill himself), part friendly and part curious, they invited him to dinner. Punctual and wearing a tie, he arrived at their place bearing three strictly identical bouquets, which each in her heart of hearts found charming. But nothing further was to come of the evening.

As for the men, most of them his superiors, he had no relationship with any, save for Gaudin, the only one who took any interest in his welfare. He was the one who showed him around when he first got to Tahas, and suggested places to shop. He was also very helpful when it came to finding an apartment. He alone had thought to give him a map of Tahas, an item that was unavailable locally for some reason, and that had to be ordered abroad from specialized bookstores. Quentin didn't forget these courtesies, and they remained somewhat friendly—but only somewhat, for Paul Gaudin was a naturally reserved man.

Every so often they went out together for a drink. Gaudin had a little goatee. He had prominent eyes, always a little woeful, and the first time Quentin saw him, he thought he did indeed look like a goat. That resemblance later disappeared, however, and Quentin found the now familiar face bore no trace of that first impression.

It was Gaudin again who took him the very first week to the Sport and Leisure Club, called SporTahas. Quentin had never much cared for sports, nor did he like sporty types in general, but certain signs indicated that he had arrived at the age when one had to start watching out, and he began the kind of serious exercise regimen he had always mocked: running in large circles around a lawn dressed in unflattering sports gear, or swimming back and forth in a pool. He made the promise that, once he had his own membership at SporTahas, he would go to the pool every day and take tennis lessons twice a week. He bought a car from a Belgian who'd had to return home abruptly. The front right door was dented, but the engine ran perfectly. An ideal car for getting around town.

A new life was surreptitiously knitting itself around him, a life made up of recent habits—hastily acquired, but already, it seemed to him, locked in place.

The coffee cup still next to the telephone told him at a glance that the cleaning lady had not come. He found the apartment in the same disarray in which he had left that morning—a livable disarray typical of many men who live alone. The French doors that gave onto the balcony had been left open, allowing dry leaves to blow inside. A film of dust covered the furniture.

Quentin went over to close the doors, saying that Yassa absolutely had to come and clean tomorrow. This was already the second day she'd skipped. It was troubling to think that she might not come back at all and that he would need to find someone else. It happened all the time. These people came from who knows where to do this kind of housework. All one knew was their first name, probably not their real one, and that was it. One fine day, they would fail to show, and there was no way to look for them, to find out why they had stopped coming, whether they had found a better job or were dead. They would simply vanish without a trace. One would then change the locks and look for someone else.

Were it not for the looming threat of Yassa's defection, Quentin wouldn't really mind her absence, for she had a peculiar way of mopping—she would throw herself onto the floor with her wet rag, scrubbing the tiles on her knees, almost prostrate at times, as if to demonstrate the full extent of her abject condition. She always looked tired and sickly, though whether this was real or feigned was hard to tell. He fell for it sometimes, feeling confusedly guilty over having somehow offended her and, to make amends, he would give her some small household object. Then, unfailingly, he would wish he hadn't.

Breaking with habit, he was going out this evening: Gaudin had asked him the favor of standing in for him at a party he couldn't attend, since he had to pick up his wife, who was returning from a two-month trip in Europe, where she'd had to go for surgery.

"So, you understand? It's a vernissage for Sanariglia's son . . ."

Of course he understood, and at that moment he'd even been glad to oblige, in return for Gaudin's many services. But when it came time to put on a suit and tie, and to slip into his socks, he could see no reason why his presence was required that night at some exhibit, at the home of people he didn't know.

He looked at his watch. It was time to get ready. A look out the window confirmed his hunch that it wasn't the sort of weather to be going out in, and that he would be better off staying at home that evening. The afternoon was waning, and it would soon be nightfall. Every evening, night came abruptly, unannounced by dusk—unless by "dusk" one meant that very brief instant when the sunless sky turned mauve. Then the city was suddenly flooded in darkness, as if somewhere an enormous dike had given way.

He had never been to the Sanariglia's, but he had no trouble understanding that they had done some substantial furniture rearranging to turn their living space into a gallery. The tables and sofas, arranged in a studiously haphazard fashion and draped in moiré silk and sumptuous satin, had abandoned their original function for the evening. The paintings, whose predominant color was a greenish yellow, were propped casually here and there. From the four corners of the central living room, loudspeakers were emitting a rather unpleasant monochord whistling sound. The lady of the house and mother of the artist moved from group to group explaining the fundamental importance of music to the visual arts. Thus Quentin realized that all the paintings represented different tunings, and that the whistling one heard was not simply the result of a faulty sound system. In the adjacent room, the hosts had spread a buffet of tiny edibles on trays and in baskets, shaped into checkerboards, pyramids, fans. He considered all this fragile, futile architecture for a moment, and decided he wasn't hungry.

Guests kept arriving, all dusty and teary-eyed, for a violent sandstorm had descended on the city. Now that enough people had gathered, no one felt any further need to look at the paintings (Madame Sanariglia herself, busy shaking hands, never left the foyer). Quentin wanted to seize the moment to make his exit. A waiter took his glass with gratitude and compunction, placing it on a tray already overflowing with empty glasses showing fingerprints and lipstick. Quentin was making his way to the door to take leave of Madame Sanariglia when a new couple entered, very different from the other people present.

The woman had felt no need to extinguish her cigarette, but simply switched it to her left hand, greeted the hosts, then immediately switched it back to her right. Her reddish-brown hair was pulled back so tight that her eyes, her smile, and her entire face seemed to be converging toward the mass of chignon at the back of her head. She was very heavily made-up, and wore an extraordinary amount of jewelry (a mix of genuine and fake, no doubt). Her escort, a man in a white suit, was wearing a splendid tie. Quentin thought that her entire person must correspond to many people's notion of beauty. Based on their age difference, they could be mother and son.

Quentin, who by then was on his way out, was the first person they met. Their names dissolved into the din of voices. The piped-in music had stopped, for a pianist who had emerged seemingly out of nowhere was now playing a piece that no one could hear. This man was overweight and getting on in years, and from where he stood, Quentin could see drops of sweat falling like tears onto the keyboard as he labored through his pathetic routine. Quentin repeated their names, almost shouting. The man in the white suit must have been Italian, since his first name was Luigi, but the woman, oddly, called him Sasha. Perhaps Quentin had misheard. The woman had a Russian-sounding name, however, which made sense out of Sasha.

The three of them made a quick exit, as they truly couldn't hear a word. Outside, the sandstorm had ceased.

Quentin let himself be dragged along to the home of some of the woman's friends to finish out the evening. There were a dozen people present, all younger than the three of them, with the exception of a man who may have been in his fifties, and whom Quentin assumed to be the host. He was wearing a palm-tree print shirt, and was laughing for no apparent reason other than the presence of the girl next to him, whose neck he fondled while whispering into her ear. His obvious desire to look younger than his years made him look older. On second thought, Quentin guessed that the man's age must be closer to sixty. Very unlikable.

Conversation was lagging. Everyone seemed to have had quite a bit to drink. A boyish-looking girl gave a self-important account of her trip down south on some humanitarian mission. That kind of misery, it's just unimaginable. And every night, you hear gunfire. They had even shot at her jeep. Quentin suppressed a yawn that made his eyes water.

Next to him, a tall, lanky American spoke in a groggy voice:

"Your bath, for instance, you take a cold one first, it's refreshing in this heat. And then, after a little while, you want to get warmer, so you add some hot water, and that feels good. But how much is enough, huh? Because if you put too much in, you burn yourself. Then what?"

Having arrived at this point of his little speech, the American lost his train of thought and poured himself another drink. Within a few moments, he had completely changed topics; Quentin heard him trying to convince the girl sitting to his left to come spend the night at his place.

"But I'm warning you, it's a pretty small apartment, I hope you enjoy doing it standing up," he said.

At that, he rose and, with no further concern for the girl, issued a general "Good night, everybody," then asked the palm-tree shirt if he could have a little bread for his breakfast in the morning. He'd completely forgotten to buy some.

Quentin, who was bored to tears, took advantage of this departure to make his own exit, and no one made a move to dissuade him.

Back home, he took out the business card he had slipped into his pocket without a glance, and learned that the woman he'd met at the Sanariglia's was named Nina Andreïevna Praskine—dance instructor—and that she didn't live on the Ring.

He would still occasionally dream of Louise. On some nights, she would come to him, soft and sweet. It was so good to be back together. She was his best, his oldest, his only friend. And in his dream, they were curled up together, talking in whispers until time stood still, and everything was explained, healed, forgiven.

He also dreamed a few times of a friend from college. They had been inseparable, then had a falling out for a reason he could no longer recall. Quentin had had his faults, to be sure, and in his dreams he acknowledged them, asked forgiveness; it felt so good to be a better person than he once was. Since he began dreaming about him, he often wondered whether Arnaud Mayeux had read this or that book, whether or not he would like this painting, that piece of music, whether he would approve of the way Quentin had left home, of the life he was leading in Tahas. He found himself taking his absent friend's judgment into account, weighing his opinions. Or again, women he had known and thought long forgotten were resurfacing in his sleep like drowning victims.

Through the open door of his dreams, these people would reenter his life during the early days of his stay in Tahas; over time, their visits became less frequent, until they finally disappeared altogether.

One morning while putting some papers in order, he came across a photograph that had slipped between some bank statements. In the foreground, houses were scattered like the gray and white cubes of some building blocks knocked over by a capricious child. They had no color except that dazzling, hard-edged white and that peculiar shade of slate gray the sea turns in stormy weather. The far horizon was scored by that day's more grayish-blue sea. It wasn't a very sharp image, but one could make out a smattering of islands, as if on one stormy day the same wind had knocked over the tower of cubes and blown those rocks out to sea. The top of the picture showed beautiful clouds scudding across the sky above the islands. This photo taken from the upper floor of the old summerhouse captured the look of the area very well. The gunmetal gray ribbon of road that went down to the sea ran past the foot of a large tree with blue-tinted foliage. Louise, visible from the back, seemed to be hurrying down that road into the distance, flanked by a large black dog. Louise's hair and the dog's coat were the same color. For a moment, Quentin was tempted to tear up the photo, then changed his mind and tucked it back into the bundle of papers where chance had placed it, thinking that nothing could be further from this world of muted, deep color than the country where he was now living and, not sure whether this idea should depress or excite him, he put it out of his mind. All that remained for the rest of the day was the fleeting and nostalgic vision of pearl-gray fog—soft, warm, and fluffy as wool.

Nina Praskine lived on the ground floor of a dilapidated house back in a courtyard. It wasn't easy to find. You had to walk through a dim passageway and zigzag around piles of garbage. Visitors were greeted by a strong smell of urine, and the first time Quentin visited her place, he almost backtracked, sure that he must have taken a wrong turn.

The house itself was not without charm, if you were willing to disregard the decrepit exterior and surrounding squalor. Fifty years ago, it had probably been a lovely suburban villa. But the city had expanded since then, and there was nothing left of the garden but a dingy courtyard constantly eroded by the helter-skelter construction of shanties made of corrugated metal and boards. An old car—who knows how it got there—was rusting away right in the middle.

The greenish-gray roughcast plaster was coming off the exterior walls in great slabs, and one could see the dilapidation spreading across the façade like a disease. One day it would reach the core of the house and the walls would collapse, at which point a fresh supply of tin and lumber would build over what was once the house.

Nina Praskine's apartment took up the entire ground floor. The two upper floors of the house were empty. The owner who once lived there had died, and his children lived elsewhere. The windows were boarded up.

In the courtyard, all kinds of people were living, sleeping, working.

"At first," explained Nina, "there was no one but the doorman and his family, which already meant a dozen people or more. One never knew exactly. Then he had his brother come up from the Azga region and move in. After that, another brother moved into the courtyard—always with wife and children—because his own house had collapsed. Add to that visits by any number of country cousins. There are always some of those around, and they stay for weeks at a time. Basically, they all make up one big family—the doorman's. You see how well-guarded I am!"

And with that, she burst out laughing.

Quentin often returned to Nina Praskine's. He never found out exactly why she'd originally come to Tahas. She'd been living there for many years, during which she watched the doorman's family grow. She'd known the place before the shanties and garbage overtook the courtyard. She recalled a lovely tree by the door—a kind of cherry tree now cut up for lumber—and a climbing rose bush in front of the house. All that had disappeared or changed, but she remained. She said she couldn't stand the weather in Europe.

In the entrance, one would often trip over one or another of the children playing on the floor. She never closed the door. Friends stopping by would enter without knocking. When she wasn't at home, they would go to the kitchen and make themselves some tea, which they would drink in the living room while waiting for her to return. Nina took no offense whatsoever. This casualness had shocked Quentin at first. Within a few weeks, he started doing the same. One felt as much at home in her place as in one's own. Mere acquaintances acted likewise, showing about as much restraint as would members of her own family. One would enter, go get something to drink, snatch a few chocolates off the buffet, and then choose a place to sit. There was always plenty to read: there were magazines everywhere, photo albums, books left wide open like birds spreading their wings, perched on the edge of a table or the arm of a chair. Nina owned a somewhat disconcerting mix of rare objects and worthless bibelots. Gorgeous antique engravings were hung next to cheap color prints. An orange plastic ashtray had as much claim to the mantelpiece as a silver candelabrum. She seemed to accept these objects the way she accepted people: as they were, without valuing one over the other.

Most of the time, Quentin would find Nina at home, unless she was out giving her dance lessons. He quickly learned to ignore the doorman's daughter, who spent her days sitting in a corner behind the coatrack. She would wrap herself in whatever clothing was hung there, bury her head in it, and sit perfectly still. Quentin gave a start the first time he came upon her draped in the folds of some sequined thing that was always glittering there in that dark corner.

The courtyard looked better if you didn't see it in broad daylight. In the evening, everything seemed cleaner, quieter. There were also fewer children. These were the off-peak hours of the day, for Nina's visitors. A pot-bellied samovar shone in a corner of the room, as if to recall her Russian origins, but she always made tea in the kitchen, because she didn't have any embers to use. Two or three cups of tea, talk of this or that, and the evening's first visitors would be arriving. Quentin would sometimes stay, but that was the exception. More often, he would try to get home early while the stores were still open, doing some shopping on the way back.

One day, she suggested he come see the little studio where she gave her dance lessons. As parents would never have consented to send their little girls to the quarter where she lived, she'd had to rent an apartment on the Ring. It was a small, two-room flat where, every afternoon from three to five, she taught the basics of classical ballet to the little daughters of the foreign colony, children of diplomats for the most part.

He returned several times, then every day at four to watch the second lesson of the day, attended by girls aged seven to nine. He would sit in a corner, waiting for the class to finish, after which he would walk Nina back to her place.

He greatly enjoyed watching the little girls dance. It didn't take him long to single out the gifted ones from among those who were less so. Nina often put him in charge of the music. Compliant and happy, he would change cassettes, rewind, and fast-forward as instructed. During her classes, Nina wore a stern expression, and liked to remind her charges that she did things the traditional way. If they didn't like it, they knew where the door was. "One, two, three . . . And one and two and three . . . One, two, three . . ." And so the children, in a momentary return to seriousness, resumed their exercises, together this time. Their limp tutus reminded Quentin of the crinkled pink petals of godetia flowers. As the tape recorder roared out the accompaniment, he found himself wishing there were a real piano on which an old spinster would relentlessly pound out the same polkas over and over.

This innocent pleasure was soon brought to a painful and entirely unexpected end. The mothers showed up one day at the studio—fortunately for Quentin at the start of the first lesson, which spared him the embarrassment of meeting them face-to-face. Imagine their surprise and indignation when they found out that a man had been coming every day to watch the little girls dance—a man in his forties, a bachelor, who had no reason for being there but might well be motivated by the most unspeakable intentions. How could you be so complacent, they asked, with the obsessions of such an unsavory individual, you of all people, Madame Praskine, the dance instructor to whom the best families entrust their children?

They demanded a guarantee that henceforth no man would be admitted to her classes, unless it be a father or uncle of one of the pupils.

When he arrived that day, Nina took him aside, into the former kitchen, now a changing room, and told him what had transpired with the emissaries she had just received. He blushed in shame at being taken for the criminal he was not. All around them hung tutus, satin slippers, children's underclothes, little tights all twisted. His gaze fell upon a grass-stained sock, which he found particularly moving. Where in all of Tahas was there enough grass to stain socks? Nina attempted to downplay the issue, and pretended to laugh it off, but it was an unpleasant matter for her as well.

He left immediately. In order to exit, he had to walk through the dance room. The little girls, strangely silent, watched him as he went, and he had the feeling their sly gazes betrayed both hostility and curiosity.

From that day on, he saw Nina only at her place, later in the day, after the dance lessons.

One evening, he found the courtyard in a state of unusual agitation. Men were in discussion, talking all at once, and women were keening.

Nina was at home, going busily through some papers, eyeglasses perched on her nose. She seemed upset.

"What's going on?"

"Libella has drowned. They've just fished her out of the water. Yes, you do know her, you know the one, the doorman's daughter that was always here, by the coatrack. Last night she went missing. Makki came looking for her, since it was very late and her father was furious that she hadn't come home yet, but she was already gone. I didn't see her leave. It was only after

Makki had left that I noticed she had taken that big sequined cape that she was always wrapped in. That seemed odd to me. Last night, everyone in the neighborhood was out looking for her. She never used to set foot outside the courtyard. I don't think she'd ever been outside, not since she was born. You've seen her, she couldn't even cross a street alone! A boatman discovered her this afternoon. He saw something shiny behind his boat, which was docked at the time. The body must have been carried along by the current, and the cape got caught in his propeller. How in the world did that poor girl, who never seemed capable of nursing the least desire, who had never even seen the Ovir, how is it she suddenly left the house and crossed so many streets to go throw herself into the river? And why in my cape? What can I say . . . ? I feel somehow that it's my fault: she was in my house, she took my cape, and she went straight to the Ovir and drowned herself."

Quentin was unable to calm her down. She continued to search feverishly for something in her desk, then in a shoebox full of papers, talking all the while, repeating that she must surely share some responsibility, that it was such a horrible thing, that she should have taken better care of the girl. That cape was the sign that she, Nina, had been the unwitting instrument of Libella's fate.

Her hands were shaking, still searching through other drawers and an old cardboard suitcase full of papers. Her cheek constantly quivering from nervous tics was painful to watch. The room was turning into quite a mess.

"What exactly are you looking for, in all this?"

"I've misplaced a notebook. My little notebook, where I write down all my . . ."

She trailed off and continued her insanely obstinate search. She finally found it in a pile of old magazines, a place she'd already looked. She let out an ah! holding up the blue notebook for which she'd searched so long and hard, then fell into a chair amid all the scattered papers and began to weep.

"Please, could you leave me now? You're such a dear, but do go home, I need to be alone. Don't be angry, Quentin, just understand me, and let me be by myself now."

He had never seen her in such a state. He wished he could do something for her, but he had to face it: he would do better to let her be. So he left for home, worried, helpless to console her. While in the courtyard, things had settled down.

By the next day, he found Nina had recovered her composure. She had put away all the papers and magazines that she'd strewn around the room, and had clearly seized the opportunity to do some heavy housecleaning. She would say no more of the previous day's distressing incident; when he alluded to the subject, she brushed it away with a sweep of her hand. The mere sight of the coatrack filled Quentin with dread, and he avoided looking in that direction. A few days later, he noticed that she had moved some furniture around: the coatrack had disappeared, and in its place she had put a little pedestal table.

His consciousness, still half submerged in sleep, whispered to him that something strange was happening outdoors. Sounds, unusual yet familiar, moved through his head in one direction, then the other, like falling stars whistling as they crossed paths. Fuzzy ideas outlined in gray rose yawning from their slumber. Cautiously, Quentin cracked open his eyes, and with a certain reluctance, observed that the room was awash in a dismal, grayish half-light that was filtering through the curtains. In a supreme effort to extricate himself from the tangled web of sleep, he now understood what extraordinary event was taking place: it was raining, and the sound of the traffic's wet wake on the asphalt Ring wafted all the way up to his bedroom.

Relieved at having identified this sound whose mystery had been making him anxious, he opened his eyes more resolutely. The vague fear he'd experienced, the muddled images of a hopeless war that surfaced from this morning's final nightmare, had completely vanished, giving way to a profound sense of well-being. So, it was raining. And with that dim light seeping in from behind the curtains came Europe—good old Europe, friendly and familiar, filling his room. But the mirage gradually faded, and things once again assumed their normal shape. It was the first rain of the season, the first rain he had witnessed since his arrival in Tahas, and that was all it was. He sat up, pulling the covers over him, and turned to the thermos on his night table, which had sat ready since the previous evening to provide the comfort of hot coffee as soon as he woke.

The sudden intrusion of Europe into his bedroom that morning in Tahas, the first day of rain, had forced him to occupy two contradictory worlds at once, creating a kind of hiatus in his existence. When he saw that misty, subdued light, which reminded him so keenly of Europe, time stood still, the way a pendulum stops for just a heartbeat. Then, the radio's droning the day's news, the warm smell of coffee, the lamp lit next to the bed, all these unimportant and comforting things grew more reassuring. Thanks to them, the great pendulum was once again set in motion.

That morning, he was even less motivated than usual to leave the warmth of his bed. It was cold and damp out. Beyond the soothing circle of light cast by the lamp, the apartment seemed like some vast, hostile territory that he now explored, mentally, discovering behind every door another icy expanse. He stretched out his arm as far as he could to switch on the electric heater, but still fell just short, and finally had to set foot on the floor. After which he jumped back into bed, shivering but cheered at the thought that the room would soon be warmer, that it was Sunday, and that he could stay in bed as long as he wanted. He lazed the morning away, warm and cozy. By the time the midday news was over, he found the room had gotten too warm and he switched off the heater, annoyed. He decided to get up.

Once out of the bedroom, he was met by the chill lying in wait behind the door, and little by little, while in the bathroom, and then in the kitchen looking for something that might pass for lunch—or for breakfast; it was an open question—his sense of well-being receded along with the warmth. He was overwhelmed now by the urge to go out, in the misguided hope that the rain would somehow restore his earlier state of mind.

This was the first time he would wear the boots he'd purchased before leaving home, on the advice of a friend. He'd had trouble imagining a Tahas that wasn't seared by the sun, and it had sounded like a peculiar idea at the time, but he packed them nonetheless, and now, all of a sudden, the formerly familiar act of slipping on a pair of boots brought back the first days of autumn as he'd experienced them as a child.

Newly booted, then, he left home with a sense of restored authority. The caretaker was squatting in front of the house, in his usual place, still as a statue. He had wrapped his head in a plastic bag and spread out in front of him remnants of some cardboard boxes to protect his bare feet from the mud. He stared blankly at Quentin's boots coming toward him, a look almost hostile in its indifference. Before he was actually aware he was doing so, Quentin stopped in front of the caretaker, something he never did. Normally he would merely nod in his direction without even slowing his pace. But this time, for whatever reason, he stopped, to his own astonishment. The caretaker looked at him without a trace of amiability. Then Quentin said hello and offered him a cigarette, which the other declined with no more than a raised an eyebrow, evincing his submission to orders from higher up, his knowledge of secrets that Quentin would never learn, and his utter contempt for this foreigner in boots. He then lowered his eyebrow back into position, his gaze fixed somewhere far behind Quentin, who was soon striding along the Ring's so-called sidewalk, furious at the caretaker and dissatisfied with himself.

There was less traffic on Sundays, but because of the rain, he had to stay far to the right to avoid getting splashed. Cars were speeding past, cutting through the muddy puddles with a kind of rage that Quentin felt was aimed at him in particular. There was no real sidewalk, strictly speaking—the Ring didn't lend itself to strolling—but rather a graveled space between the garden fences and the pavement. Quentin's new boots were spattered with mud now, and his trouser cuffs were soaked. He felt the morning chill cutting a path into the depths of his interior. Every passing car projected a wave of muddy water that landed just short, like lead shot. The rain was still coming down, but it was a cold drizzle now that looked as if it might last for days, one of those rains that would end up erasing all the works of mankind from the face of the earth.

Above the city, the sky was a dull, uniform gray. He noticed he was walking much too fast for someone just out for a stroll: his bad mood and the chilly weather had combined to quicken his step. Mortified, he slowed down. Because the cigarette refusal incident had troubled him, he'd completely missed the stairway near his building that led down to the Low Road. He had to take the next one. Oddly enough, this was his first journey outside the Ring with no particular destination in mind. The metal steps shook beneath his boots, which by now had lost their shine. Recalling the look of the caretaker, he was secretly glad they had. The Low Road, which basically tracked the upper Ring, only one story down, had been plunged into darkness. The traffic passing above made a continuous rumble that, together with the vibration of the iron pillars, sounded like a machine shop in some vast hangar.

Once his eyes had adjusted to the dimness, he could make out lightbulbs dangling here and there. Dust had accumulated around the wires, turning them into thick, disgustingly hairy stems that seemed to belong to an intermediary kingdom between plant and animal. The bulbs themselves gave off only a sooty, low-watt glow, leaving large pockets of gloom. There were few cars, but the streets were choked with bicycles, donkey carts, and itinerant merchants wheeling their wares. Around every pillar, little stalls had been built, and grafted onto each stall in turn were shanties and lean-tos made of sheet metal, bits of plastic, and cardboard. On that day, the area was particularly crowded with people come to seek shelter from the rain. Quentin had to cut through a group of children playing, and fearing they might hit him with their ball, quickened his pace. Just in time, the eldest intercepted a throw that would have struck him in the head, and the group watched in silence as he passed. The kid then said something that made the whole gang laugh, and Quentin could hear the snap of the ball being passed from hand to hand behind him.

But, overall, people paid no attention to him. Men standing around seemed to be waiting for something, collars raised against the damp. They formed small, dusky groups speaking in hushed tones. At one point, it seemed to Quentin that they were growing more numerous, and he got the feeling that something was wrong. This must be what it's like in times of civil strife, when the atmosphere gets heavy, right before a riot breaks out. He imagined the moment when people would start running, as others stooped to pick up stones. There would be black smoke everywhere. But it was only the rain that had brought all these people down to the Low Road. No violence in them. Minds blank, they were waiting the way one would at a train station. The very notion of impatience was foreign, the concept of future unknown.

Seated on a mat, a woman was selling oranges and watching people go by. Quentin's eyes met her voracious and mocking stare. She was wearing a brightly flowered peasant dress, and in this colorless crowd, she and her pile of oranges shone like the sun.

She sold him a small bag, charging him the rich man's price and flashing a toothy smile that displayed all her gold crowns.

Quentin resumed his walk, strolling distractedly, head bent over the open bag as he breathed in the scent of the oranges that girls must have picked joyfully, hastily, grabbing pell-mell at fruit and leaf with soft rustling sounds, and he could see their own flowered dresses drifting among the trees like summer light through branches. After all, somewhere beyond the city, there had to be true countryside with fields, orchards in bloom come springtime, the distant barking of dogs in some barnyard. There were certainly men sitting somewhere on a grassy slope, foreheads dripping with sweat as they rested a moment before picking up their scythes and getting back to work. Out there, you hear the clucking of chickens and the braying of donkeys, country cousins of those city donkeys that are used to haul away garbage. And the crickets singing in the dry grasses. And at nightfall, clouds of mosquitoes rise into the mauve air, and frogs make croaking noises in their ponds.

He reached a sort of intersection where the Low Road branched off from beneath the Ring: back out in daylight—a light the color of pewter—he continued on his way, eating oranges as he went and breathing in the smell of their crumpled leaves. By force of habit, he was careful to keep the peels in the bag, unable to make himself toss them onto the street. Then he left the bag full of peels and leaves on a pile of slow-burning garbage that was giving off an acrid smell.

Across the street, he spotted one of those big state-owned stores open on Sundays, and went in for no particular reason. Once inside, he was immediately struck by how depressingly ugly the place was. To the right of the entrance, an obese young woman was snoozing away in the bedding department. That day, the only item for sale was a scratchy-looking bedcover in brownish gray, the kind they must give out in prisons. Above her, a neon light was blinking relentlessly. Elsewhere, shelves were sparsely stocked and spaced in such a way that Quentin felt a little lost in the vastness of green linoleum that covered the entire ground floor. For want of anything better to do, and to feign having some sense of purpose, he went up to the next floor, where the women's apparel department featured grim house-dresses and nightgowns in a pathetic floral pattern. Above a pile of dreary undergarments, by way of advertisement, hung an oversized pair of panties. He began to wonder what in the world he was doing there, and promptly exited the store. The rain had stopped. Above the roofs, colorless clouds sped across the convalescing sky as it emerged pale blue.

He walked and walked, turning onto streets at random, sometimes right, sometimes left. He walked through several more or less lower-class neighborhoods he had never visited. One street led to a public garden whose rectangular shape appeared on no map he had seen. It was a small park whose brick-colored paths took up more space than did the lawns. Women were strolling with their young children, showing them the caged monkeys, which seemed to be the local attraction.

Quentin sat down on a bench, resting his tired legs. He watched all those children gathered around the cages, those families picnicking a short distance away in a patch of weeds, shielded from the damp ground by bits of waterproof sheeting, and he felt utterly depressed. He didn't know whether to feel sorry for himself or for those women with their big, filthy feet in cheap plastic sandals. For that matter, he had always been unsettled by that sort of thing—families out in their Sunday best, or floats covered in crêpe-paper flowers. Or by those russet-tinted photographs of families having lunch out in the garden, everyone staring into the camera with a gentle, vaguely questioning look. Slender young women turn their heads in surprise toward you, the viewer. They are sitting up very straight, as if they feared the chignon balanced on their heads might roll off and fall to the ground like fruit. That their silhouettes would stoop with age and their enigmatic sepia smiles disappear forever distressed him as much as any outright disaster.

Overwhelmed by the bleakness of it all, he got up from his bench and made his way toward the exit. At the gate, a uniformed employee asked him for his ticket. It had never occurred to him that payment might be required for entrance into this humble park. Disinclined to argue, he pulled out his wallet where he found no small change, only bills of large denomination. The ticket taker didn't have change either, and let him go with a shrug.

Quentin had no idea where he was. He'd made his way haphazardly thus far, unmindful of which streets he was taking. He now regretted this inattention and wished he could get home as fast as possible, without having to take these same unfamiliar streets, without having to cross through these same unrecognizable neighborhoods. He picked up his pace, his despondency having vanished, his only concern now being the long trek back. No taxis ventured into these lower-class neighborhoods. Finally, after a good hour of aimless walking, he happened upon the banks of the Ovir where he least expected to find them. It was already nightfall. In the distance, further upstream, he recognized some tall buildings, and concluded that he must be far south of the Ring. At least he could get his bearings now. He paused for a moment, leaning against the balustrade to gaze at the water and the illuminated riverbanks. Occasionally, a black clump of plant matter flowed by like a bouquet, a dark spot against the iridescent current. He walked north along the river until he reached a large, bustling square where he immediately found a taxi. The railing had left a bar of dust across his chest, and his hands were dirty.

It was already late when, grim-faced and with eyes set straight forward, he strode quickly into his building, determined not to turn his head toward where the caretaker usually sat.

He was still on the stairway when the power went out. He decided he had better forego loudly stamping his boots on the steps, and cautiously crept up the last flight to his landing. He felt around a long time before finally getting the door open, and again, once inside, before coming up with candles and matches. At last he managed to affix a candle to the cracked saucer he set aside in the kitchen for just that purpose. Power outages were quite frequent, and each time, Quentin vowed to buy a real candlestick, then promptly forgot all about it. He sat on the little chair in the hall next to the phone, and waited. The streetlamps out on the Ring were lit, so the apartment wasn't in total darkness. In a city this size, even late at night, it was never truly dark. In addition, all the shutters were broken. He had raised this point with the landlord, back when he had first arrived, but the man had just looked heavenward: "Of course they are, they're very old. But as long as you don't touch them, they should hold a bit longer. And in any case," he added, "we can't fix them, since they don't make that kind anymore." After an initial flash of indignation, Quentin resigned himself to inaction. All in all, better to have them always open than always shut, and so, day and night, the shutters gaped.

The phone sitting next to Quentin also seemed to be waiting. The roundness of the receiver shone in the chiaroscuro like the shoulders of a doll. Suddenly, simultaneously, light was spilling over him and the phone was ringing. He jumped, heart pounding. There was no one at the other end.

His pulse still throbbing, he blew out the candle and carried all three items—candle, saucer, and matches—into his bedroom, in anticipation of the next blackout. When he switched on the bedroom lights, he saw two large cockroaches scurry away, one under the armoire, the other under the chest of drawers. There was no hope of catching the second one. But the armoire's feet set it quite high above the floor. Down on all fours, Quentin could see the immobilized insect up against the baseboard, seeming to stare back at him. Having now located the bug, he went to get insecticide. By the time he was back, however, no more roach. It was always the same. These vermin were so exasperating. But tonight he felt particularly depressed at the idea of sleeping in a room where two cockroaches lay hidden. Two? It was conceivable that as soon as he switched off the lights, an entire population of cockroaches would come charging out from under the armoire toward the chest of drawers, and from there to the armchair and onto the bed. In a rage, he took aim and fired his bug spray under the bed, under the armoire, under the chest of drawers, under the chair, then waited. Seeing no further sign of a cockroach, hostilities ceased.

There must have been other power outages throughout the day: nothing in the refrigerator was cold, and the ice cubes had almost completely melted. He was disproportionately distressed by this, as if by the sight of some other calamity on a much larger scale, one that involved him directly, as both victim and perpetrator. He drank a glass of water and returned to the bedroom. In the middle of the room, an overturned cockroach was in its death throes, fleshy insect thighs waving in the air. With a mixture of disgust and contentment, Quentin tossed it in the trash.

None of this was particularly gratifying. It crossed his mind that he should move out. The apartment was too big for him. Ever since the weather had begun to cool, the place felt uncomfortable. There was always a draft. And the wood of the door-frames was starting to warp, as was that of the closets and all the doors. Nor would any of the windows properly close. Wind blew through all the gaps and whipped through the full length of the apartment. It was as if a stranger had somehow forced his way in, and Quentin no longer felt at home. But moving wouldn't solve the basic problem, he thought. His weary mind attempted to define what he himself meant by "the basic problem," but drew a blank. He concluded that perhaps he needed to take a vacation, and felt relieved at having found such an ordinary and reassuring explanation for his anxiety.

With the onset of winter, Tahas became increasingly grim. Quentin had enjoyed the early days when the cold first descended on the country; after the brutal summer, he experienced genuine relief to feel once again the shade of clouds moving across the land, like a cool hand on a sick patient's forehead. Summer there was like a fever that left the earth cracked and thirsting for water. For a short time in early winter, the country still bore traces of summer on its parched skin, so that the first gentle rains came as a kind of resuscitation.

But with time, winter seeped into the core of all things. It was cold outside and in, and no wall could keep out the damp. The locals, both men and women, wrapped themselves in large brown woolen shawls. Yassa now invoked the cold to excuse her absences, just as she had invoked the heat only a few weeks earlier. The intermittence of her work mattered less now that there wasn't as much dust, so Quentin refrained from comment. He simply decided to pay her only on Saturdays, to be certain that the housework would get done at least once a week. And he would occasionally do a little sweeping himself.

To get to Nina's, he really needed to wear boots. The courtyard was a morass of muddy puddles. Planks had been laid end to end leading to her doorstep, but the ground below was uneven, and the boards wobbled underfoot, forcing visitors to advance with caution, arms spread for balance like tightrope walkers. A family of cats guarded the door. They had settled on a pile of rubble and kept still as statues. Quentin discovered their presence only gradually, balls of beige and russet hair, all curled up, looking surly as they watched people pass.

One evening, a man was pounding a piece of scrap iron near the house. The barbarian clang resounded against the walls, its echo so mournful that Quentin felt suddenly disheartened. There was something desperate about the man's dark silhouette, as if, for some unforgivable crime, he had been condemned to perpetual exertion. Behind the man, wood was burning in an old oil drum that served as a makeshift brazier, and beyond this little patch of light, everything seemed plunged into immeasurable darkness. Quentin thought of a campfire, the night of a lost battle. Nina had drawn her curtains; not a ray of light filtered through. A lightly acrid smell of burning things floated in the air.

He found her seated beneath a lamp, busy darning some woolen stockings. She had put on her glasses, and looked like the old crone in some fairytale.

She looked worried. Sasha had written again asking for money; he was threatening suicide. He was sick, she wasn't doing anything for him, she was abandoning him. Always the same thing. He lived in France, almost never came back to Tahas. He had a boyfriend there, she knew all about it. Had known for quite some time. A fellow who calls himself a painter, but who's never completed a painting, and who spends his time drinking in bistros on Sasha's tab.

"Everything my father left me is melting away, thanks to that deadbeat. Because Sasha can never say no to him, and I can't say no to Sasha, you see how it works. I'm always so afraid he'll do something stupid, and maybe because of me, if once, just once, I don't give him what he's asked for."

She imagined that Sasha survived only because there was someone in the world who truly loved him, with a total and disinterested love, and that any failure on her part in this duty would lead to his misfortune and demise. Against this fear, she imposed a kind of superstition on herself, a promise to keep ever-present in her heart the image of this man who was never there and who didn't love her in return.

She felt so alone here, deprived of his presence, at such a distance from him. And those horrible letters he wrote her; though, better those than none at all. As long as he was still writing, nothing irreparable had occurred. Perhaps someday all would be put right again, and he would finally understand. Anything was better than his silence, which is why she kept sending him money, a bit like buying the right to observe him and his lover at a distance, in all their pathos. Could it be that they would remain ever thus, tied to one another yet separated, like three stars in the same constellation? After all, money didn't mean much to her. It wasn't money she'd earned, after all. If she denied it to those in need, she felt it would somehow bring her back luck.

Outside, the hammering had ceased.

She went on: "You know, I have a little house in France. I inherited it from my grandmother, who lived in it nearly her whole life. When I'm old, and once I've had enough of Sasha, I'll go live there. I'll have time to think. I've always said that one shouldn't finish out life in a hurry, don't you think?"

One ought not dwell too long on that small dark fault that lies waiting at the end of life, she thought to herself. It's there, growing a little wider by the day, and most people approach it backward. And when that most anticipated day does finally arrive, they are like small animals still pulsing with life, staring wide-eyed with fright at the hunter hovering above, so startled to see the chase cut short. Which is why the existence of that house where she never visited proved a comfort at bleaker moments: that is where she would go to live out her days. She would live just as her grandmother had. In the morning, she would get vegetables from her garden for soup. After which, she would head back down to the house and sit a moment on the bench by the door. The sun is nice on that side of the house, sometimes: sun that warms like a smile, not like the searing sun of Tahas. She'd sit there a long while, watching her garden grow, then go inside and make her soup. During her expedition into the vegetable garden, the cat will have followed her, striped fur wending its way between the carrot plants like a tiger on the prowl, crouching among the ferns. Perhaps she would also have some rabbits, to which she would make a daily offering of tops and peels, later in the morning, once the soup had begun to spread its fine fragrance throughout the house.

This was how she saw herself, and while dreaming out loud of this humble happiness, she could forget Luigi Garullo.

"Speaking of rabbits, have you ever seen Makki's?"

She coaxed Quentin outdoors after throwing a large brown wool shawl over his shoulders.

Makki wasn't at home. Nina shouted his name all over the courtyard to no avail. The man who had been hammering his piece of iron was gone. The bits of wood in the oil drum were now dying embers.

She took Quentin by the arm and led him to a dark corner near the passageway that led in to her house. Without hesitating, she pushed open a kind of door—just pieces of cardboard cobbled together and attached to the fencing. A small lightbulb hung from a wire and gave off a yellowish glow that strained the eyes.

This was Makki's domain: an area measuring at most two meters by three, with rabbit cages stacked floor to ceiling. Each hutch housed a seething furry multitude that, in the dim light, looked like grayish magma. There were hundreds of them, curled up against one another. Upon closer inspection, once one's eyes adjusted to the cave-like dimness, one could make out throngs of flattened ears, quivering noses, a large wet eye here and there. Incessant motion spread through them like shock waves, causing a constant undulation of the furry gray surface. There was something fascinating about rabbits in such numbers, and Quentin and Nina both stood a long while gazing in wonder through the wire mesh of the cages. An analogy with the caretaker's family could hardly be avoided.

A young man entered without saying a word, and he also watched the rabbits. He was wrapped in some sort of dark cape that made him look tall and slim, which he most probably was. He gently tapped one of the wire cages to get the attention of the rabbits inside. Nina asked him where Makki was. He had no idea. Then, still without looking their way, he stooped, opened one of the smaller cages, and removed two newborn rabbits that he displayed on the palm of his hand, two little bodies, rosy and naked as a fetus. Quentin wanted to hear a little squeal, just to be sure they were alive. It was a disgusting sight.

With the index finger of his free hand, the young man stroked the little creatures, just barely a caress, then placed them back in the cage from which he'd taken them, down low, and when he stood back up, Quentin noticed that he was exceptionally beautiful. Skin very dark. But Quentin didn't have time to get a better look; the young man barely glanced in his direction before nodding good-bye to Nina and making his exit without a word.

"That's Ghazi, Makki's brother."

But the name was no help to Quentin in explaining why this face had troubled him so. There was something hard about the young man's physiognomy that made him think of an idol—extraordinarily fine features chiseled into granite. Unless the impression came rather from the vacant look in the young man's eyes as they met his. This hardness didn't fit the more feminine cast to his face, nor the grace of his movements. Back at Nina's, Quentin sensed in himself the persistence of a slight irritation, and thought that he absolutely had to see the young man again. He had rarely encountered anyone so beautiful.

For once, no visitors had yet arrived by this hour. The cold and mud had perhaps discouraged them, so Quentin lingered a bit longer. He drank a glass of cognac to warm himself while munching on some crackers that happened to be there.

He asked Nina whether it was hard to find a place to live in her neighborhood. He was fed up with the Ring, where he was always running into his coworkers, and his apartment was too big, too poorly designed, too cold. The draftiness was making him sick. In fact, he was having health problems more often than before, never anything well-defined or alarming: headaches, dizziness in the morning, and intestinal troubles. Nothing very original. Was there anyone in Tahas who didn't experience minor ailments like these?

"It's true, you're not looking too well these days. You should take some time off, but you should stay on the Ring."

"And why's that?"

"I don't know, it's just better."

"What about you?"

"I'm a different case."

He felt a little annoyed that she should cast him out like that, onto the Ring with all those people he had so little to do with. He would have liked some encouragement (of course, my dear Quentin, you're not the kind of person who lives on the Ring) instead of being told that he should stay put in a world that she herself had so long ago abandoned.

He got home very late that night: right when he had wanted

to leave, it began to rain again. So he stayed a while longer at Nina's, waiting in vain for the rain to stop. It was almost midnight by the time he made up his mind. It might rain until morning, and it made no sense to wait any longer. One glass had led to another, and they ended up drinking quite a lot of cognac. Quentin, all warm by now, couldn't imagine why he had let a few raindrops keep him from venturing out. Determined, he strode straight across the courtyard, disdaining the path of wooden planks that the rising waters would soon set afloat.

With each step, he heard the gray pebbles crunch beneath his feet. He tried his best not to crush them, but he couldn't do otherwise, and it was upsetting to step on all those tiny round stones that cried out beneath his soles. He couldn't hear what they were trying so hard to tell him—he was so much bigger than they. He purposely took large strides so that he would step on their faces as little as possible. They had all at one time been flesh-and-blood creatures like himself, until that day when their foot had slipped into one of those evil slits that lie waiting for us all, hardly visible on the ground. They then fell screaming into that slit no wider than a finger's breadth, reduced forever to little ashen pebbles—but all had kept a face and a soul. And he, the only survivor of a bygone world, walked across this desolate field, and he was afraid, afraid to crush those gray eyes, those open mouths, so afraid of his foot slipping into one of those slits that lay waiting for him, no larger than a finger, because there was inevitably one there, and he knew it, into which he would fall screaming, reduced forever to an ashen pebble.

He woke in a sweat. It was two in the morning. The bedroom was cold; he had to make an effort to stop his teeth from chattering. A fever, perhaps? Oh yes, the rabbits, of course, that was it.

In his fitful, shivering sleep, he thought that Nina must have been right; he did need to take some time off.

The Palm Beach was the only hotel in Azga. There were two or three other addresses in the town center near the market where one could sleep, but it would never occur to any foreigner to spend a night in such places. Quentin saw one of them from the taxi window as he crossed through town. A narrow stairway, looking more like a ladder, climbed straight up and disappeared into a kind of subterranean darkness after the first few steps. Above the entrance, a sign written in French in a childlike script, red lettering against a yellow background, proclaimed "Hôtel des Roses."

The taxi driver stopped at the entrance to the Palm Beach, but made no move to get out and open the trunk. Slumped over the steering wheel as it channeled the engine's vibrations to his thick hands, he waited. So Quentin went back himself and fished his travel bag out of the vast trunk, deep and dark as a bread oven, and lined with old, grease-stained rags. The driver gestured toward the meter with his chin, then watched with a nasty look as bills left wallet.

Entering the lobby, Quentin was dazzled by the brightness of the sea that glittered behind the huge plate-glass window. He had come into a vast, white-walled, high-ceilinged hall, where there was almost no furniture, no pictures on the walls or carpets on the tiled floor. The overall feeling was one of such emptiness that Quentin was surprised to see a hotel clerk behind the reception desk, watching him as he approached. His jacket gleamed white against the dark wood panel behind him where the keys hung. At least two or three hundred, estimated Quentin, and not a one was missing.

When the man asked him his name, there was a moment of

hesitation that allowed him to follow up, this time with a hint of reprimand:

"You did make a reservation, sir, didn't you? No? Oh dear, this is quite awkward, you see, we never give out rooms without a reservation, Sir. I don't quite know what . . ."

He left his sentence unfinished, hanging there between them like a falling leaf. When it hit the ground, the clerk made a perfunctory show of paging through a fat registry, his welcoming smile now gone for good.

"I shouldn't think it'd be a problem. I'm guessing that you have quite a lot of empty rooms, this time of year," Quentin quipped, gesturing jovially toward the full panel of keys.

The other made no reply and seemed totally absorbed in contemplating the columns of his registry. At a glance, Quentin was able to read upside down that the registry was open to July. They were now in January. It then occurred to him that perhaps the fellow didn't know how to read. He was on the verge of insisting they give him a room and be done with it when another young man arrived on the scene, almost running. He must have been wearing taps on his soles, for his steps could be heard at quite a distance. "Hello, sir," he blared. "Welcome to Azga!" "Zga," went the echo from the bare walls.

The new arrival turned to his coworker and, in his own language, fired off a few words that struck like daggers: the other let go of the registry, seemed to literally slink under the counter, then backed away from the desk and disappeared.

"You must certainly be Mr. Corval, am I right? Don't worry, everything is in order. Madame Clara stopped by in person a couple days ago and asked that we reserve you one of our finest rooms. I hope you'll understand my colleague, who must not have understood who you were. Madame Clara left a message for you, actually."

He handed him a little blue envelope that Quentin refrained from opening there in the lobby. With one ring of the bell, another character emerged from behind a partition to take the bag. He walked so quickly that Quentin had trouble keeping up. As soon as he had opened the door to the room, the porter disappeared without leaving Quentin time to dig for some change.

He went to open the drapes to have a look outdoors. There were palm trees. He would have to have a look around, he thought. For the moment, though, he wanted to read that letter.

He grabbed his bag to set it on a little table, realizing in the process that there was a streak of axle grease all along the bottom. He tried to remove what he could with some toilet paper, but only managed to get his hands dirty. After scrubbing them for a long while under the faucet with one of those tiny hotel soap bars, there remained only a brownish spot on the index finger of his right hand. It reminded him of those rolls of licorice they'd given him as a child, which he detested. He put his bag on the balcony and took the letter out of his pocket:

> *Our mutual friend Nina Praskine wrote me a short while ago asking that I reserve you a room in Azga. This is not always easy to do from Tahas, but it's so easy to do for someone already here! I'll stop by the hotel the evening of your arrival to make sure everything went smoothly. I'm looking forward to meeting you. See you soon.*
>
> *Clara Vair*

Now that he held the key to what had seemed an enigma, he

was disappointed. His bad mood, only latent since his arrival, was starting to express itself more fully. He was furious. Why couldn't he just be left alone? This whole reservation question was absurd. There were at least three hundred rooms in the hotel, all apparently empty.

He went out for a walk around the premises. A sandy stretch planted with palm trees separated the hotel from the beach proper. Apart from a few scraggly bushes, nothing grew in the bare ground. The desert extended right up to the gates of Azga, and its presence was palpable. All along the shore, they had built little huts covered in palm fronds. The wind had left them all in bad repair. A crab emerged from its hole right in front of Quentin, but quickly retreated, frightened. He'd had just a second to glimpse its pinkish-white legs, which made it look like a hand. He put his sandals back on. At one end of the beach, he saw columns reaching toward the sky like the ruins of some ancient temple. It was an outdoor cinema. A large blank rectangle stood facing the sea.

Quentin went over and sat in the very back, on a bit of low wall. He sat there a long time staring at the solitary screen, its back turned to the marine horizon. He had trouble imagining that a film had ever been shown here. Rather, he saw it as a bizarre monument erected on this beach to represent "The Absurd" or "Absence" or some such abstraction.

He felt chilled by the wind, and resumed walking back to the hotel. The waves were rough and deep-voiced, accompanying the scratchy rustle of palm leaves.

When he got to the pool—a little basin, empty now, its walls filthy—he saw coming toward him a woman dressed in red. He was immediately struck by the way she walked. She held herself very tall, her neck appeared endlessly long. She seemed to glide along the ground, dancing her way toward him. He noticed she was wearing red flats, like a ballerina. Or a toreador.

A chunky silver bracelet glistened on her tan wrist. They shook hands and went into the hotel lobby, where crystal chandeliers glowed from the ceiling. Quentin had just enough time to watch the sun, fatally wounded, sink into the flaming horizon. Clara's dress took on an almost supernatural luminescence and seemed to retain, within its folds, some of the blood-red afterglow of the dying sun.

Images of the end of the world passed through his mind as he was talking to Clara Vair, and he felt gradually suffused by a pleasant excitement, which he attributed in good faith to the splendor of the sunset.

His fears were unfounded: Clara had no other plans for that evening and was perfectly free. She had laughed when he asked.

"Is there something in particular you think I should be doing at night here in Azga?"

What had he been thinking? That the nightlife in Azga was such that she had invitations to go out every evening to receptions and events? She no longer enjoyed even simple dinner parties among friends since she moved to Azga. No, no, nothing like that, she was absolutely free.

"But of course, I don't want to impose. Coming from Tahas, you probably just want some peace and quiet."

Her manner was a bit hesitant, and she took a step back, her smile quickly fading. She'd made overtures that she regretted now, and felt she'd rushed things with this total stranger—a friend of Nina's, but still . . . And on her lips he could read something like chagrin.

This upset him, and it showed. So she took pity on him: they would dine at the Brazza. They had great shrimp, but there was also meat, if he didn't like seafood. Oh, but he adored seafood. He really did, and shrimp especially. And they were suddenly back to their cheerful selves, relieved at having resolved that momentary dissonance.

They would meet up in an hour in the hotel lobby.

Just as the Palm Beach was the sole hotel worthy of that name, the Brazza was the only restaurant anyone would recommend to travelers visiting Azga. There were other establishments claiming to function as restaurants, but no way on earth would anyone risk actually dining in such places: wobbly metallic tables resting unevenly on a floor covered in wood shavings; wooden chairs black with filth, as if charred in a blaze; tabletops stained with interlaced circles, the pattern growing more complex as each day wore on; sugar crystals glittering like mica beneath the raw light of fluorescent tubes; streaks of cream and crumbs left on plates where flies would come feast; and at night, the last customers would linger, crouching in their brown woolen wraps, feet on the rungs of their chairs, chins on their knees, looking like owls. Never a woman in this sort of place.

It was too chilly, of course, to dine on the terrace. There was only an inky darkness out the windows, but the sea continued to exert its spell on the diners: the few customers that evening had all chosen tables right next to the bay windows. Though there was no view of the sea, they could at least enjoy the cool air gusting through the loosely fitted panes. Clara headed straight to the back of the dining room and chose a table in the corner.

They had run out of shrimp, but the grilled fish was just as good. Sure, he'd love to try the grilled fish. He hadn't really wanted the shrimp that much anyway. She laughed a little, then there was a moment of silence. This often happens in a restaurant in the evening. You were looking so much forward to going out to dinner with her, with him, and once at the table you've chosen, or even reserved, your enthusiasm starts to wane. It's been a long day, you suddenly feel exhausted. You've summoned your last bit of energy to order the meal, and now you're waiting to be brought the wine, slumped over, grim-faced, feeling you've aged considerably since just a moment ago, as if an evil spirit had draped your shoulders with an invisible cloak of weariness.

But it didn't last: there, it's already gone, their conversation resumed, and with a little help from the wine, they began to laugh. They talked about Azga, about Tahas, about her job.

They also talked about Nina, and Clara laughed as she thought of her letter. It was clear that Nina thought she could use a little company, and generously sent this other loner her way. You can never tell. But Clara naturally kept these thoughts to herself.

"And you never come to Tahas, even though it's so close?

His voice had an imploring quality that she found touching. It was hard with only one day off a week, and there were times she was on duty—even though her turn came up only every third time, she still wanted to be available, just in case. As director of the Azga branch, she felt responsible.

It was getting late, or at least that was their impression, since all the other tables were cleared, the customers gone, and the lights dimmed in the entrance. Since the service was rather slow, they decided to have coffee at Clara's place.

The next morning, Clara arrived late for work. She had left him the keys to her house. He could stay with her as long as he wanted. Since she was a foreigner, no one would look askance at her behavior here, so he shouldn't worry. After she had left, he stayed in bed nearly an hour more, curled up in the warmth of the bed, idle, breathing in her scent on the pillow. He saw the set of keys glimmering on the nightstand and found them grandly symbolic.

It was so cold in the kitchen that he was tempted to take his coffee back under the covers, but he felt like going out, and didn't want to spend the whole morning in bed. He also had to go back to the hotel to get his things and pay the bill. Might as well get that over with.

The cat came and circled its dish, finally deciding to eat.

Quentin made some overtures to it, but got no response.

The rather chilly reception he received at the Palm Beach made his mind up not to have a last walk on its beach. He stopped by Clara's to drop off his bag, then was off for a stroll along the sea.

Not far from the house, fishermen's wives were selling fish under awnings made of palm fronds. The sun filtered through the dry, interlacing leaves, and below, the white-bellied fish sparkled bright silver in the shifting light. It was cold, the sky was a deep blue, and the wind rustled the palms.

He got the notion to surprise Clara, and bought some fish. The initial goal of his walk, which was to have no goal at all, was now modified: he walked away from the sea and started looking for the market square, which he had passed the previous evening. (Was it only last night? It seemed so long ago now.)

He came back with two bags full of fruits and vegetables. It had been quite a hike, but he was happy that morning to walk in the sun and to know that Clara would be there to eat with him.

They were very lucky with the weather. It was chilly, but almost always sunny, and around noon they could even sit outdoors, provided they were sheltered from the wind. There was a little bit of garden right up against the house that was protected by a low wall. Once the sun arrived on that side, Quentin brought out a wicker chair and settled down for an hour or so with a book he'd found on Clara's shelves. It was lovely out, with insects buzzing around in the greenery. There were all sorts of flowers with tiny orange and mauve corollas. From time to time, his gaze would fall upon an ant climbing up a stem, a hovering bee, a butterfly flitting above the grass. Butterfly white, fine weather in sight. Quentin stretched a bit, sighed in contentment as he cracked his knuckles. Then he plunged back into his book, while waiting for her to get home from work.

On Sunday, they went to visit the ruins of Garazdar. Clara had made inquiries: she found out that the road had been reopened, and that despite extensive damage caused by the recent rains, the route was passable.

They packed a lunch. At the bottom of a basket, Clara laid a bottle of Italian wine that had been waiting months for just such an occasion. She also included, wrapped in a neatly ironed checkered napkin, some cheese and fruit. Quentin wedged this perfect basket between his legs for the journey.

To leave Azga, they had to drive through the slums. Clara drove very slowly to avoid splashing people as she navigated the puddles. Here and there, goats grazed on garbage, untroubled, while a bevy of ducks waddled past. Everywhere there were dogs, cats, chickens, all kinds of country fauna that turned the city into a barnyard.

For the next fifty kilometers or so, the road headed due west, hugging the dips and rises of the rolling terrain. With every lull in their conversation, Quentin felt overcome with sleepiness, and nearly dropped off several times, rocked by the alternating hollows and crests. He would be jerked back into consciousness whenever the car hit a pothole, to hear Clara apologizing, visibly annoyed at not being able to show off what she considered her excellent driving skills. To their right, the sea shone like sheet metal.

They arrived at a miserable jumble of huts. The few boats on the beach were the only sign of human activity. The place did have a name, though, and the previous evening, looking at a map, Clara described it as a fishing village. Quentin had imagined whitewashed houses, fishing nets stretched along the beach, and a little café with wicker chairs on the dock of a tiny port, water lapping gently at shore.

Once past these lowly buildings, the road went under a kind of brick arch, a pathetic construction marking the exit from—or entry into—the village, after which it forked. To the right, it followed the sea, curving northward. The road to the left, the one they were to take, led into a mountainous mass that, at a distance, seemed very low, a flat line on the horizon.

As they drove closer, the mountains gradually rose, and behind Quentin and Clara the sun rose in a cloudless sky as if driven by the same force as the emerging mountains. Shades of color became increasingly distinct across the landscape, with the sea now intensely blue, while veins the color of purplish-red porphyry and sulfur ran along the rocky surface.

The road then got very bad and began a steep rise via a series of hairpin curves hewn right out of the rock, passing through gorges, passing alternately at every moment between sun and shade. Every so often, a solitary tree would appear, an enigmatic reminder of vegetation.

Clara parked the car on a graveled roadside overlook created for that purpose. They continued on foot in single file on the narrow track along the rock face. It was very cold in this shaft of shadow, where the sun never shone. The sky seemed far away, a tiny celestial river that ran far above their heads, through which the black arrow of an occasional raptor would fly. The powdery path absorbed the sound of their footsteps. Neither of them felt like saying anything, so powerful was the silence. As they emerged from the narrow path and into the sunlight, the contrast came as such a surprise that they laughed, as if a joke had been played on them.

They found the landscape extraordinary, with its smooth,

pink boulders, as gentle to the touch as to the eye, and its series of pools filled with green water. Like a couple of children, they were thrilled by the strangeness of the place. They picked out a nice flat rock for their picnic. The stone was warmed by the sun and wide enough for them to stretch out side by side. Quentin had the urge to take a swim in the water of these marvelous natural pools. They began undressing, dipped a leg into the emerald water, which felt icy cold, and remained half naked for a while, wavering on the edge of the basin, feet frozen and faces aflame. They should come back in the spring, when it's not so cold. In the summer, this rocky wilderness would become a veritable furnace, with the gemlike water reduced to stagnant, unwholesome-looking puddles.

After lunch, they got dressed again and continued walking along this row of rose-colored basins. The ruins of Garazdar soon came into view at the foot of a slope. The remnants themselves were a disappointment: pillar fragments scattered on the ground, like the pearls of a giant broken necklace, along with a few blocks inscribed with inscrutable characters. They wandered past more inscriptions, deaf to these centuries-old messages crying out in the stony solitude. They only had eyes for the splendor of their natural surroundings, which in turn were indifferent to their presence.

They arrived home after dark.

He stayed a whole week in Azga. And then two more days. Of course, he should have let the consulate know that he would be absent longer than expected, but the very idea of picking up the phone seemed too much to bear. He had no acceptable excuse and was far too old for schoolboy ruses. But, more than that, he simply did not want to think about returning to Tahas.

The morning of his departure—he did have to leave, in the end—the weather was gray and mild. Clara went to work a little early to avoid the traditional farewell scene. (When travelers have already placed their suitcase on the train and picked a seat, securing their spot with the magazine just purchased at the station's newsstand, hands now free, they get off the train for just a minute to say a last good-bye to the person who accompanied them, and this last minute goes on forever, as everyone knows: we are better off avoiding that minute in which speechless lovers watch as the nectar of their brief affair spills onto the station platform.)

In any event, Quentin didn't go home by train: there was no station in Azga. The fastest way back was to take one of the group taxis that served the Azga-Tahas route. A vehicle with one seat still available was about to leave when he arrived, so there was no wait. Drivers shouted their destinations out the window. Everywhere, people were scrambling to reach the vehicle that would take them away from Azga for the day, for a week, perhaps forever. Others, looking more like emigrants, were waiting crouched next to their baggage: cardboard suitcases bound with string, large baskets of provisions, burlap bags bursting at the seams.

A little girl in a scarf and flowered dress was carrying a basket of lemons. She was holding it on her hip, exactly the way the women here would carry their babies. She wended her way between the vehicles, knocking on closed windows or slipping her little beggar's hand inside when she found one open. She already seemed old beyond her years, and was so dirty that Quentin felt heartsick. Then the taxi drove off, and he left Azga taking away as a last image the timeless face of the little lemon vendor.

PART TWO

It was most likely evening. The window was casting a lunar glow, partly onto the upper wall, then angling onto the ceiling—the electric moon of the streetlights down on the Ring.

He must have slept quite a while, since it was only mid-afternoon when he'd dozed off. Light poured through the window, projecting strange, moving forms onto the wall. It was entertaining to watch. What could it be that was producing this dancing shadow? He concluded it must be a street sign swaying in the wind in front of a streetlight. On the fourth floor, though, that was hardly possible, was it? He mused a moment over what else might be the cause, and how much he would love to see the trembling shadow of the leaves of a chestnut tree. He envisioned a little square somewhere in Europe with a fountain in the middle and the stately chestnuts all around (they could also be plane trees). And he, by chance, would be staying at an inn located right on that picturesque square, with its paving stones and arcades, and it would be called the White Horse Lodge, or The Sojourner's Inn. Travelers would be served hearty country cooking, washed down with a robust red wine. And on the walls of the dimly lit dining room would hang gleaming copper pots and the mounted heads of stag and boar.

There he would be, stretched out in his cozy little bedroom, after dining copiously under the watchful eyes of the hunting trophies, and he would watch the leafy shadows flitting softly across the ceiling.

Ah, this headache . . . damn this climate! As soon as Quentin switched on his bedside lamp to look for some aspirin in the nightstand drawer, the magic lantern where he had seen an inn somewhere in Europe was extinguished.

The apartment was a dirty mess. Zina had been coming for a while, then disappeared. One day, Yassa had begun groaning that she was too old, that her legs ached, that she couldn't work anymore, and in her place, she inflicted Zina on him, her daughter, supposedly. Were it not for the clutter and filth that was starting to take over the apartment, he would have been delighted never to lay eyes on Zina again. She must have been all of fourteen or fifteen. She kept her shoes on while she cleaned—a pair of worn-out high heels, two sizes too big, which made a constant racket on the tile floor in the hall. She was dirty and always made-up like a whore. He avoided looking at her filthy nails beneath their chipped polish. In fact, she might well be a whore. She often acted a little odd, with that dubious smile of hers. Ever since he had fallen ill, shortly after his return from Azga, she stopped showing up. The apartment was a depressing sight, and he was too sick to clean it himself. Maybe tomorrow.

He had slept enough, and so kept the lamp lit. He lay on his back, staring at the ceiling, trying to recover the thread of his thoughts. Where was he? Oh yes, the arcades, the chestnut trees, the inn, and what else? In the dining room, for example, there would be a huge brick fireplace. Would there be a fire burning or not? Since there were still leaves on the trees, it wasn't the season for lighting fires yet. On the mantel, a little clock stuck at ten minutes past four, its pendulum motionless for eternity. The waitress, in black with a white apron, would bring glasses, a bouquet of them in each hand. Through a swinging door, we would be able to glimpse the whiteness of the kitchen. Something vaguely repulsive about that beauty mark just above her lip. And who had been along for the hunting party where that stag met his death? Some of the hunters who had risen early on that morning—the fields were still drowned in fog—were themselves now dead, perhaps. How do people enjoy hunting? It was one of Gilles's passions. No reason why that should have changed. I'll bet she goes along with him, she probably enjoys hunting just as much. She must think it's exciting to wear big boots and to carry a rifle, emblems of brutality, yes, she probably likes that. Gaining admission into a male world. And she likes getting up early, which is good if you hunt. Brutality, yes, that's exactly it. They're two of a kind, in the end. Even as a child, there was something brutal about him. In the shape of his mouth, maybe: big, thick-lipped? Even his curly hair made him look violent. And it wasn't merely a look, since no one could ever get the better of him. His years at boarding school resolved nothing. When he would come back home, Aunt Cathy didn't know which way to turn: so, it was his favorite dishes, and little presents under his pillow, and soon pocket money, far too much money. He used swear words I didn't understand. At that age, a year's difference means a lot. We used to fight so much back then, the two of us. He usually won, but not always. Once, I made a bloody mess of him, with Aunt Cathy screaming all the while. Nina was shocked the other day when I told her it was too bad I hadn't simply killed him off back then. It would have been the perfect opportunity. It wasn't possible after that, of course. I don't like thinking about him, but I think about him all the time anyway. And not only because of Louise. It goes back further than that. All those magazines he used to bring home, that he was too young to be reading. He would show me pictures of nude women. My tentative expression would make him laugh. And the day he slipped a few of them in one of my notebooks. In class, the pictures fell out onto the floor, in front of everyone, and I wished I could leave school and never go back. And on top of all that, he was a good student. Surprising, isn't it? A good student doesn't get into fights, he answers politely when questioned, doesn't hide pictures of nude women under his mattress. Sometimes I wonder how the two of them act when they're together, I have trouble picturing them. They called the kid Stéphane. It didn't take them long. So Gilles has become a man, cradling his son. There must be times when he's gentle, in private, like everyone else. Oh, to be six again! She used to make me warm milk with honey. Good for the throat. Nobody left to call me her "little teddy bear" now, I guess. Damn, it's cold! This awful fever . . .

He rose to his feet like an old man, sighing ostentatiously for no one but himself. It took him ages to string his bathrobe sash through its loops, then he had to stoop down to search for his second slipper, which had gone astray under the bed. When he stood up, his head was spinning. He went into the hall and picked up the phone, with the vague intention of calling a doctor. He stood there for a moment, undecided, frowning with exhaustion, then put the receiver back down.

In the kitchen, he found a little jar of honey way in the back of the third drawer down. On the cap, there was a laughing bee and the name of the Grand Hotel. What ever possessed him, knowing he didn't particularly care for honey, to slip this tiny jar into his pocket as he was leaving after breakfast on that now remote morning of the first day of his vacation? It would have been almost a year now. An eternity. He broke three matches attempting to light the stove to heat a pan of milk, and thought that must be bad luck. No, it was the other way around: using one match for three cigarettes. Which war did that come from, anyway? He turned off the gas just in time, the milk ceased its bubbling, leaving a white veil along the inside of the pan as it descended.

He had heated a little too much. He looked, puzzled, at the milk left over in the pan—barely a half cup's worth—and thought how practical it would be to have a cat. Why hadn't Clara written? Unless she had, and the post office had just interfered . . . He'd heard that domestic mail often got lost.

He began to sip as he wondered how long it had been since he'd had milk with honey in it. Thirty years, at least. This was the taste as he remembered it (and the last sip almost bitter it was so sweet, thanks to the honey that remained in the bottom of the cup). Would she take care of him if she were here? Maybe she would make him milk with honey, but "my little teddy bear," no, most certainly not. Nobody. Never again. What had those ruins been called again? There was a Z in the name . . . They put them everywhere here, Zina, Azga, Ghazi—where had he met someone by that name?

He put the sticky cup in the sink with the rest of the dirty dishes, and the bright sound of clinking porcelain made him start.

He dragged his feet back into the bedroom, humming a tune to accompany the music of his slippers. Two notes, flip, flop. The only one who might call him that was Nina, of course, Quentin my little teddy bear. Go to sleep now, my little Quennie-bun, my little Quentin.

His fever was spiking again.

When he left his apartment for the first time to return to the consulate after an eight-day absence, the weather had shifted. The unkindly cold of the previous weeks was ready to move on: as if overnight, it unshackled both man and beast, and was gone. One fine morning, the country woke surprised to find its cell door open and the warden nowhere in sight. When had all this happened? Quentin had remained confined to his room for eight days, doors and windows closed, keeping the cold air inside, without knowing what was happening outdoors. And there he was, walking along the Ring, savoring the incomparable sweetness of the first steps of his recovery. The sun high above looked like a jolly old king and, on earth, everything was milder, more tender.

His car was parked a little farther on, which gave him another fifty meters or so to walk. Everything was new and worthy of love. He felt moved by the sight of the scrawny hedges of greenery behind the garden gates and discovered for the first time little red berries on the potted bushes. Everything had recovered a certain substantiality: everything was more sharply outlined, the uniform haze of winter had given way to clouds with bodies as luscious and firm as flesh. Sun had restored the world's third dimension. Could it be, Quentin thought, that all our moods are nothing but the reflection of the light or dark clouds passing above our heads?

As he passed through the consulate gate, he wished he was still stationed in his office in the little annex out in the garden. Recent remodeling of the buildings meant that he'd lost his privilege of seeing a little greenery every morning. From his new window, he could now see nothing but a section of wall and a bit of sky. At least there was more light than before.

On his desk, he found more paper than usual, the result of his eight-day absence. Nothing from Clara. He settled back in to work, feeling as if he'd been gone for weeks. All these application forms, all these passports seemed more foreign to him than ever. He wondered whether this feeling would fade as he got back into his routine, or whether something had really changed, and then he remembered that he had decided to move out of his apartment. The idea had occurred to him several times, but these last eight days had convinced him that he needed to find something smaller, to get away from Zina, to get off the Ring. Nina would surely help him out. All those folks in the courtyard would certainly know if there was something available for rent in their neighborhood. Gaudin didn't know anybody outside the Ring, but Quentin would ask him anyway, on the off chance.

White clouds passed over his azure bit of window and disappeared behind the section of ochre wall.

There had been vociferous complaint over the color of the new roughcasting, but Quentin rather liked this saffron tone, which reminded him of certain Italian palazzos. Rosemonde Goult had simply shrugged it off, rolling her eyes. No use insisting. Gaudin didn't like the new color either, but he at least knew what Quentin meant: he would have preferred that reddish color, that mix of earth and blood one also sees in Italy. Quentin decided to go see Gaudin right away.

His office door was wide open. He had stepped out for a moment, so Quentin waited, having a seat in the chair facing the desk, the one reserved for visitors. On the wall were some antique engravings in gilt frames: a map of a city curled into the loop of a river, an early eighteenth-century map of France, soldiers in uniform—white, blue, red—sporting plumed shakos and carrying bayonets.

A rigorous order reigned in this workspace. In a little frame set at an angle in one corner of his desk, Jeanne Gaudin smiled.

It was only later that he regretted having gone to talk with Gaudin. He hadn't understood Quentin and they almost got into an argument—no, not an "argument," really, one doesn't argue with a man like Gaudin, but Quentin did sense that the man was a bit annoyed.

Gaudin, like everyone else, had the preconceived notion that one could not, should not live outside of the Ring. But why not? Gaudin didn't know a soul beyond the Ring. Still, that morning's encounter made Quentin feel like an eternal adolescent, a kid being lectured by his father. He emerged feeling mildly resentful, while at the same time knowing that Gaudin only wanted to prevent him from doing something he might later regret. It had been a long talk. In the end, each stuck to his original position, and they parted, mutually disgruntled. At several points, Quentin thought he saw flashes of that fleeting resemblance to a goat that had struck him when they first met. He noted as soon as he saw him enter the office that Gaudin seemed concerned about something. Everyone has bad days. At that point, he should have simply postponed the conversation. He decided to go talk to him again the next day, certain that their little misunderstanding would get cleared up in no time.

That's what he told himself as he made his way through the passage that led to Nina's courtyard—a few meters of the dense air, thick with shadow and stink (the hovering odor of garbage, echoes of the stench embedded in the walls against which neighborhood men and dogs would come relieve themselves). They weren't so much walls as ramparts, and he couldn't shake the early impression he'd had of entering a medieval fortress. The courtyard, where there reigned a cloistral silence at this hour, seemed turned in on itself, connected to the outside world only by this filthy tunnel where several times he stepped into some unidentifiable soft matter, and where he suddenly forgot Gaudin and what had ensued between them, as if, like a path leading to an enchanted kingdom, this passageway had the power to erase the memory of all who crossed its threshold.

The days were growing noticeably longer, so that even though it was the same time of day as usual, bits of twilight gold still clung to the net of sky. But it was already dusk in the houses here, and there was light in the windows.

Nina didn't have a telephone, and since she abhorred the device in any case, she wouldn't even make use of the phone at the little post office practically next door, so that Quentin had gone for over a week without hearing from her.

The door was open a crack, and on pushing it open, he understood that she was going away.

The big black trunk had been taken down from atop the armoire where it had sat for years, and was now in the middle of the room, funereal, lid wide open as if for a wake. Quentin just stood there looking on for a moment, reading the stickers like so many epitaphs of days gone by, adorned here and there with a palm tree, a sun, a pillar from a Greek temple against a yellow, green, or blue background. *Coral Beach, Barcelona, The Ambassadors, The Lido Hotel, Athens, Venice* (several times, Venice), *Aix-les-Bains, Singapore*. Singapore? She had never said anything to him about having been to Singapore. In any event, none of that proved she had actually been to all those places. The stickers looked rather old, most of them torn in places.

There were still other names, like *Lufthansa, Iberia, Adriatica,* that all sounded like a women's names. The black lacquer had grown dull with age and was all cracked, flaking off in places. It was one of those old-fashioned trunks that perhaps had once belonged to a solitary wanderer of an uncle who aroused a passion for adventure and postcards among his nephews, whom he hardly knew; and later, this same trunk, rediscovered and brought down from the attic, cleaned and touched up with paint, had been sent off to Tahas on the trail of an unknown niece, a half-Russian who had inherited her uncle's wanderlust. Unless she got it from that grandmother she'd told Quentin about one day, the one that left home as a young girl in the last century to teach French to some mischievous, daydreaming Natasha. (On her way, she must have imagined vast frozen forests, troikas dashing between the birches, whose sleigh bells could still be heard long after they had passed, as if the horse team had flung pearls of sound to the wind, ringing out, rolling down the snow-covered slopes. As she left Berlin, it was starting to snow, and perhaps she was sinking into sleep as she watched the country-side turn white, and in that half-slumber where nothing seems surprising, she dreamed she saw large golden bubbles flying out of belfries into a snowy sky.)

The papered walls revealed pale phantoms of the pictures that had been taken down. Quentin made a game of trying to recall what had once hung where. He had to admit defeat several times and search for the answer among the pictures that were still sitting around the room, on the floor or up against a chair. He was able to reconstitute all the décor with the exception of a place to the right of the fireplace, where a mysterious medallion had left a small oval shape; he came up with nothing, neither in his memory nor in the cluttered room. The overall effect was one of walled-up windows, or patches of emptiness scattered about, the immaterial remains of things that were no more. The only item remaining was a calendar hanging on the kitchen door. The samovar was set on the floor next to the trunk.

She had removed the piece of fabric that once covered the sofa, making an indecent display of the pathetic olive green plush underneath, with its mess of stains. She had carefully folded the fabric and placed it in the trunk: a simple rectangle of big orange flowers resembling roses and dahlias set against a bluish-black background, which would soon be elsewhere, covering other sofas in other houses in other cities. Cardboard boxes of all sizes had sprung up in every corner of the room, like a bloom of beige and gray. Everywhere, linens and newspapers. She had put out a half-smoked cigarette in a saucer—Quentin could see the slick purple imprint of lipstick on the gold-ringed filter—and had abandoned a teacup three quarters full on the credenza.

In the kitchen, everything was dirty and grease-stained. The garbage pail under the sink was overflowing. The tiles felt sticky underfoot. No way to make coffee.

When he turned around, she was framed in the gilt of the mirror, frozen, like an ancestral portrait. Her image lingered, but the real Nina was already gone. And she may have had a similar impression when she saw Quentin leaving the kitchen, centered in the door frame, the full-length portrait of a stranger. She was momentarily startled, then their images left their respective frames, and they met up in the middle of the room. *What? You were sick? Really? Oh, my poor Quentin, I wish I'd known!* And if his illness had lasted a little longer, would she have bothered to come see him before leaving? Those are questions best left unanswered, and he was simply glad to have recovered in time.

She seemed much calmer now that she had finally made up her mind. She'd been torturing herself for weeks about whether or not to leave, always coming up against the same question. Everything made more sense now that the deciding was over, and this long-dreaded departure now seemed the obvious choice. What would she really have done with that house? She never went there, and there was no guarantee she would ever get to live there one day. Anyway, it was over now, she'd sold it, no use thinking about it anymore. And there would even be money left over, once all Sasha's debts had been paid. She'd probably find herself a place in Paris, or rather the suburbs, it was less expensive there. She wouldn't need anything fancy. At any rate, it would be better than continuing to live apart like this.

Quentin stood there, not quite knowing what to do with himself. All the chairs were piled up with her belongings. He said nothing as he watched her continue to place things in the trunk with swift, precise little gestures. The light would occasionally glint off a brilliant in her ring. A family heirloom, no doubt. She must have come across it while sorting through her things, because he'd never seen her wear it before. The sight of her sparkling hand darting about made him wonder why it was that he had always felt so sorry for her. There was a short silence, and he sensed that she was expecting something from him.

"So what about you, what have you decided? Since you're not going to stay in Tahas forever, I assume?"

No, of course not, he wouldn't be staying forever, but neither was there any sense that he would be leaving any time soon. He was there, waiting, with no real expectation of anything happening, not even quite sure what this could be, an event, a sign he would recognize when he saw it, upon which he would know that the time had come for him to leave. He would settle right back into the life he had left behind (his job at the consulate certainly wasn't holding him back), so there was no hurry, he could take his time: a month, a year, ten years, time meant nothing to him, really.

Still, how strange it is, he thought as he watched the ring going back and forth into the trunk and out again, in-out, in-out: she's really going away. He had trouble picturing her anywhere but tucked away in this courtyard where she had practically become a patron saint of sorts, a healer whom everyone in the neighborhood came to consult, innocently confident in the virtues of her medicine cabinet, where she would reach in and produce pills to relieve toothache, syrups to lower fever, powders to calm a child's stomach pain. And now she was leaving, chasing after this Sasha who didn't love her—and he was surprised to find he envied her.

"Don't give me that look! I didn't mean to put you on the spot. Come on, let's polish off this cognac together. There's just enough for two glasses."

She went into the kitchen and brought back two stemmed cut-crystal glasses. She held them up to the light to make sure they were clean, then emptied the bottle into them, taking care to equitably distribute the last drops.

"There. These glasses used to belong to my parents. There were once more than a dozen, but I broke so many that these are the only two left. You can have them as a souvenir; that way, you'll think of me whenever you drink from them. You can have the books, too. I left the key with Ghazi, you can come see if there's anything that interests you . . . Cheers!"

The two glasses touched with a pathetic little clink. He felt like asking her whether her house was already rented. He thought he might take it for himself, but he didn't dare raise the matter, for fear of seeming rude. He was genuinely upset to see her go. He could always ask the caretaker once she'd left.

"I almost forgot: I got a letter from Clara Vair. She sends her best wishes. She's leaving for good this time. Her father can't live alone anymore. She'll be leaving Azga at the end of the month.

She glanced at the calendar still hanging on the kitchen door.

"The twenty-eighth, that's today, isn't it! My, how time flies . . ."

He helped her put things in order, setting everything she was taking with her in one place, near the trunk, and what she would be leaving behind over by the wall.

She removed a white satin tutu from one of the boxes. The tulle was torn in places and had yellowed somewhat. She held it out by the straps, the way one might hold a lantern, and she eyed it for a moment, swinging it gently back and forth. Then, she put it on top of the boxes that would be staying in Tahas.

There was nothing edible left in the kitchen, and in any case, she had already given away all her pots and pans to the caretaker's wife. They decided to go get dinner at a little eatery she knew not far from there, a working-class restaurant that was also clean, a rare sort of place in Tahas. It was there that they said their good-byes. Nina left two days later, very early, and didn't want Quentin to take her to the airport. It was nice of him to offer, but there was no sense dragging himself out of bed at that hour just to give her a lift. And anyway, truth be told, she always preferred to be alone at times like that.

He went back to Nina's the very day of her departure, as if to convince himself that she had left Tahas for good. He was also anxious to check whether her house was still available.

Before entering the passageway that led into the courtyard, he realized that he didn't know exactly which shack Ghazi lived in. He wasn't even certain that he lived in the courtyard, since Nina had mentioned one day, in passing, that he didn't live with his family. And he wasn't often seen around there, in fact. He felt something resembling panic at the thought that he might lose all trace of the kid. He had just enough time for the feeling to sneak up on him, but not enough to delve any further into why he'd felt it.

Ghazi was there. He was leaning up against a junked car, smoking a cigarette. With face tilted toward the sun, he slowly exhaled the smoke, blinking his eyes. He looked focused, nasty. He was wearing tight blue jeans and a gray checked shirt open at the chest. The season no longer called for large brown woolen shawls—which Quentin had never actually seen him wear in any case: in the winter, Ghazi would always go around in that black cape, in which he seemed to take great pride.

As Quentin moved toward him, Ghazi put out his cigarette and came forward to meet him. One might have thought he was expecting him. He took a set of keys out of his pocket and, without a word, opened the door.

The bare walls seemed to have spread apart. Emptiness reigned. Quentin had imagined that they would sit there for a while, maybe on the sofa, and smoke a cigarette together, reflecting on all those awful, trivial truths: the passage of time, lost friendships, etc. But Ghazi remained standing next to the door, just watching him, waiting for him to finish whatever he was doing. The daydream was over. To recover his composure and justify the visit, Quentin set about examining the books Nina had left behind: dictionaries, maps, volumes of poetry, *Complete Short Stories, translated from Russian (Vol. II)*, no author name. He spent a moment paging through some old magazines that lined the bottom of the crate. He felt self-conscious and thwarted. So as not to leave empty-handed, he took *The Child of Taganrog*, whose red leather binding appealed to him.

The other had just been standing there this entire time. Quentin wished Ghazi had taken a stroll rather than staying put, as if to keep an eye on him. Quentin wanted to linger a bit longer. As a stalling tactic, he offered a cigarette, which the other accepted, unsmiling, with a nod of the head. Quentin had one as well, and went on perusing the shelves. At intervals, he tapped his cigarette above the orange ashtray that she had not deemed worth packing, and which continued to advertise the superiority of a particular brand of alcoholic beverage to the empty apartment.

The objects he had helped her sort only two days before were still in the back of the room. He looked them over distractedly, not much interested in any of that. On top of one of the boxes was a burlap bag. He looked inside and found Nina's old white tutu. He didn't want to take it out in front of Ghazi, but decided without really knowing why that he would bring it home with him. There was certainly no one here who would know what to do with it—not that he would either—but there was something funereal and old-fashioned about it that appealed to him. Nina had once showed him some newspaper clippings in which she could be seen wearing a tutu, with her name in all capitals: *Nina Praskine*. So he piously rescued this relic of her bygone glory, taking care to keep the bag tightly closed.

The courtyard people had clearly gotten to the kitchen before he did. There was nothing left. Even the boards she'd used as shelves had been carried off. Only the calendar featuring a Swiss landscape had failed to find any takers. It hung there on the door, frozen forever in the month of March, like an unwound watch.

While lighting a second cigarette, he dropped his box of matches, which promptly slid under the sofa. He didn't like the idea of getting down on all fours in front of Ghazi, although by this time, tired of watching his every move, the kid had turned to look out the window. Quentin pulled the sofa away from the wall, which required a certain effort, and recovered his matches. On the floor, up against the baseboard, he recognized at once the blue notebook for which Nina had once spent an entire day searching. It had slipped back there unnoticed, and she had forgotten all about it. He shook off the accumulated fluff, which fell softly back to the floor.

Only the first few pages had been used. It was a list of names, sometimes only first names, each followed by the name of a city and a date. The most recent read:

Libella, Tahas—4 October 199–

And he thus concluded that she had recorded the names of deceased friends. All these names had once appeared among the names of the living, in phone books, in address books. When their numbers were called, they came and picked up the phone, they read the letters sent to them. And, though surviving just a bit longer than the actual persons, all these names eventually disappeared from files, phone books, lists. The copper plates above their doorbells and on their mailboxes were changed. And in no time, yes, in no time at all, their names were also erased from living memory. Nina hadn't had the heart to cross out the names of these friends, nor to refrain from copying them into her fresh appointment book for the new year that would unfold without them. So, she had devoted to her dearly deceased this notebook that she had chosen, in a sky-blue cloth binding that suggested nothing morbid.

He slipped it into the bag with the tutu and the copy of *The Child of Taganrog*, and let Ghazi know that he had finished.

The young man had not stopped smoking this entire time. He tossed the butt into the fireplace, stepped aside to let Quentin pass, then closed the door behind him.

When the time came to separate, they had yet to raise the issue of whether the house was for rent. Unexpectedly, it was Ghazi who broached the topic first. He explained in broken English that the place was not for rent because the owners had sold it. He added that he, Ghazi, could help Quentin find something else in the neighborhood, if he wanted. How did this kid find out he was looking for an apartment? Nina must have said something; yes, that made the most sense.

They set up an appointment for the following morning. It was a holiday, they would have all morning and afternoon, which, according to Ghazi, was more than enough time to find an apartment in this neighborhood.

"So, have you heard the latest on Corval? He's leaving his apartment on the Ring and moving out someplace, I'm not sure where, near the meatpacking district I think, anyway, that's what I heard. Honestly, I can't imagine what he thinks he's going to find out there that's better than the Ring. He's the one who's always complaining about cockroaches. Well, he'll get more than his share out there. What in the world's come over him, do you think? Unless he's gotten involved with somebody from that neighborhood, but believe me, if he's starting to hang out with the local women, he's in for some surprises! I heard he won't even have a telephone out where he's going. I know what you're thinking: an old bear like him doesn't want a phone anyway. Well, stay tuned, there'll be more to this story, I assure you. Remember last time, when he didn't come back from his vacation in Azga? And I was already saying: well that's it, we won't be seeing him again. So he came back in the end, you say. Four days late and not a word of explanation to anyone. He's got a lot of nerve, I'd say! Over at Parker, I'll bet you anything that he must have got into some trouble right from the start; I'm thinking they're the ones who let him go, and not the other way around. You can't work with thugs like him. I don't know how Gaudin puts up with the guy. Poor man, I really feel sorry for him. This will be his wife's third operation, you know. She has to be near the end this time. The other day, I went into his office to bring him some files, and he was crying. I don't know how long he'll stay with her. If things don't improve, I can't imagine he'll be coming back any time soon. Life stinks sometimes, doesn't it! And speaking of health, to get back to Corval, he's not looking so good these days, is he? He looks sick. These unmarried guys, they never last long at foreign postings—unless they play for the other team, if you get my drift. He doesn't look like one of those, but you never can tell, can you? Maybe he's having a little fling with a butcher from out at the meatpacker's, whaddaya think?"

Unlike his former apartment, this one was unfurnished. Quentin had to buy a bed, a table with three chairs, and an armchair. It was wicker furniture, locally produced, not bad-looking and very inexpensive. The kitchen was equipped with the bare minimum: there was one of those three-ring gas stoves found in every kitchen in Tahas, a big refrigerator with rounded contours like the ones they used to make thirty years ago—very noisy but in good working order—and a buffet.

He moved into his new lodgings barely a week after finding the place. He turned in the keys to his Ring apartment with such a sense of relief that he felt as happy and relaxed as after a swim in the sea. He'd feared all sorts of recrimination and quibbling over scratched furniture, a stain on the carpet and other petty details, but the owner proved understanding and indifferent.

He had been warned that power outages were even more frequent in these neighborhoods than on the Ring. He got a demonstration on his first day. The power went off in the afternoon and didn't come back on until very late. Night fell on the neighborhood like a candlesnuffer.

He lit the hurricane lamp that he had wisely purchased that very morning, and spent the evening in his wicker armchair watching the giant shadows of two of his chairs flickering on the wall (the third served as a nightstand), listening to the noises welling up from courtyard: the clang of pots and pans, the plumbing's gurgle, an infant crying somewhere. All these sounds came to him as if from afar, dampened, filtered by the silence of his room. The sounds were very different from the ones he used to hear on the Ring. Here, only domestic noises could be heard, living noises that people were making at home as they went about their business: cooking, rocking one child while chiding another. Cats vocalized their loves and hates, and their fights made the metal steps of the service entrance shudder. The ruckus they caused provoked helpless howling from a dog down in the courtyard. But all these greatly muffled sounds had something peaceful about them that reminded him of the countryside. Finally, if he strained, he could hear the desperate bleating of animals at the slaughterhouse, located not far from his building.

On the Ring, he could never hear anything but the racket of car horns and the incessant dull roar of their engines, the city's basso continuo.

The lamp set on the ground cast a raw light on objects, throwing disproportionately large shadows onto the walls. There was something odd about such a stark white inside the apartment. This kind of lantern reminded him of nights spent outdoors, in a countryside buzzing with insects and night creatures under a starless sky. Archeologists must use lanterns like these in the evening, as they rest outside their tents, not far from their dig, their faces illuminated by this miniature beacon, their backs turned to the circus of the night. Were they still digging at Garazdar, he wondered. He regretted not having paid much attention to the ruins. But at the time, he was more interested in Clara than anything else. There were a number of sites to visit in this country. On the outskirts of Tahas alone, they had come upon tombs decorated with magnificent frescoes. Who knew what might remain to be discovered? He should get interested in all that; it was exciting. He would go the next day to the Institute of Archeology, which was located on the Ring, a short distance from the consulate. It was housed in a rambling old villa, recognizable at a distance for its neo-Gothic style. It would feel good to read some old history tome in the library that he imagined must smell of citronella and furniture wax. Yes, that was where he would spend the hot hours of the day from then on, settled into a place near a window, always the same desk in dark wood. Outside, the sun would be lurking like a wild beast, looking for a way to break in, hurling itself against the wall, gnawing at the threshold. A fresh, green half-light would sift through the Venetian blinds, and all around him would be nothing but books with their antique gilt titles looking on in silence. He could also purchase a few. They could be found, if one looked hard enough. No later than tomorrow, he would go have a look at the International Bookstore, where there were a few works available in English. He would also need a good reading lamp, so as not to strain his eyes.

The shadows on the wall were starting to look like horned creatures. Exhausted by the austere pleasures of erudition, he dozed off.

It was one in the morning when he woke, shaken from his fitful sleep by the brutal light of the ceiling lamp: the electricity was back on.

Quentin was quite pleased with his new lifestyle, and had no regrets about leaving the Ring. He didn't miss Nina at all, oddly enough. The only thing he was still fretting about was his last conversation with Paul Gaudin. The next day, he went and knocked on his office door to talk things through and dispel the previous day's misunderstanding. He had intended to be especially friendly, maybe even to apologize. He'd thought about inviting him to lunch at the Metropole. They hadn't been back there in ages.

But Gaudin wasn't in his office, and when Quentin inquired about him, Rosemonde Goult looked at him as if he'd fallen off the moon. So, he hadn't heard? Mr. Gaudin had left the previous evening. His wife was having her third operation for cancer, and the news wasn't reassuring. The woman was dying, to put it bluntly. Goult couldn't believe he hadn't heard!

So that was it: while Paul (he would call him Paul from then on) was getting ready to rush to the bedside of his dying wife, Quentin had been complaining to him about how drafty his apartment was, how the windows wouldn't shut all the way and how often he caught a cold as a result, how inconvenient the floor plan was. He'd grumbled about the high ceilings and how hard it was to heat in the winter. And to finish up, he'd launched into a lengthy indictment of the Ring and the people who lived there. He cringed in shame now at the mere thought.

He started hanging out in a little neighborhood café at the corner of the street leading to the meatpackers' and a little alleyway where spare car parts were sold. Even at high noon, it was dark in this alley because of the sheet metal awnings above the stalls. The clang of hammering on scrap metal could be heard all day and late into the night. Beneath the awnings hung bunches of hubcaps, exhaust pipes, rearview mirrors.

He entered the café almost by chance, during one of his exploratory strolls right after he'd first moved into the neighborhood. He was struck by the name of the establishment: Café du Port—in French. A waiter was serving what looked like nicely chilled bottles of a local beer, and this enticed him to enter.

He sat down in a remote corner, conscious he was being stared at, and ordered a beer. And as he leisurely drank, he tried to imagine what dreams or memories had inspired the owner when it came to naming this desert-bound café in the middle of Tahas, so far from the coast. As he turned this enigma over in his mind, he felt something like a tidal wave of nostalgia and a yearning to walk along the docks of a port. He began to dream of topsails, of the poop decks and forecastles of yesteryear. The local beer was stronger than it looked: his dreamy wanderings in the South Seas came to a stop, settling on the lovely word "parrot," all raucous and plumed.

Ghazi had just entered the café, preceded by a few other young men. They sat down in the opposite corner, and Quentin ordered a beer for all of them. It was immediately apparent that, among his group of friends, Ghazi was the leader. He gave off a gang-lord aura.

The proprietor—it had to be the proprietor, that heavyset, weary-looking fellow over there—the proprietor, then, climbed down from behind his counter, abandoning the cash register, which, until then, he had been guarding with his life, and went in person to serve the young men. He spoke with Ghazi, gesticulating broadly and laughing loudly, and Ghazi half-grinned while looking around him, his mind conspicuously on other things. His gaze met Quentin's, though too fleetingly for Quentin to acknowledge him with a nod, for Ghazi's eyes continued to scan, neither lingering nor accelerating, but pursued their circling motion, steady as a lighthouse beacon.

The owner cut the conversation short and went off to get a rag, as someone had knocked over a glass. He wiped the table with great diligence, then the one in front of Ghazi as well. He berated the waiter, who vanished, then returned in a flash with a new bottle of beer and a clean glass. Still talking, the owner served the one who had knocked over the glass, taking great care not to let the head overflow. He who a moment ago reigned in majesty behind his cash register was now bowing obsequiously to speak with these kids. He looked so servile that Quentin wondered whether he wasn't somehow afraid of them. But that made no sense: most of them were basically children, whereas he was a mature man, proprietor of a café that must be well-known in the neighborhood. Afraid of what?

He returned to the Café du Port a few days later, then starting going back every evening. The same faces were always there, give or take a few. Each time, at about the same hour, the little Ghazi gang would show up and go sit in the same corner. And each time, they were entitled to the same deference on the part of the proprietor. They would often have a game of tric-trac, clicking their tiles as they played. Ghazi never took part, though. He would merely watch the others with an air of superiority ("If that's your idea of fun . . .").

It wasn't too much longer before he stopped acting as if he didn't know who Quentin was, and they would simply nod to each other. Hello. Hello. That was all.

One day, Quentin wandered into the Café du Port in the early afternoon, not his usual hour. The proprietor wasn't there. There weren't many customers. Flies darted about feverishly, crazed by the sticky puddles at the bottom of glasses.

Someone was sitting in Quentin's customary corner, watching him walk in. As he moved forward, his eyes gradually adjusting to the dim light, he saw that it was Ghazi. Quite naturally, they found themselves sitting face to face.

They ordered coffee, and Quentin lit a cigarette, to have something to do with his hands. They hadn't spoken since the day they had looked for an apartment together. In the evenings since, at the café, they only ever exchanged nods, the vaguest of greetings, keeping their distance like people who only know one another by sight and intend to keep it that way.

Right off, Ghazi asked him in his halting English whether Quentin knew of anyone who needed a chauffeur. He was out of a job, and didn't want to do anything except work as a chauffeur. Cars were his passion. He was asking Quentin in particular, since he probably knew lots of foreigners, and he wanted to work for foreigners. They paid better. He preferred Mercedes, incidentally. He mentioned that in passing, on the off chance there would be a choice of car. You never knew.

No, unfortunately, Quentin didn't know of anyone. (And even if he had known someone . . .There were always ten applicants for every slot. And then, Ghazi would have to learn some languages if he wanted to work for foreigners. But Quentin kept these thoughts to himself.)

Then, out of the blue, Ghazi asked whether Quentin could lend him some money. It wasn't really a large amount, but it wasn't trifling either. Quentin took out his wallet. He happened to have a fair amount of cash on him that day. As he counted out the bills, he felt both uneasy and happy.

With a barely audible thanks, Ghazi stuffed the money

into his pocket. Then he put out his cigarette and left, after gratifying Quentin with an appreciative nod. As he watched him walk out, Quentin had to admit that the guy had style. He wore his insolence well.

The ants made their entrance into Quentin's place overnight. He discovered their shiny, black column as he was getting ready to heat the water for his morning coffee (his thermos had broken during the move).

They were coming from a corner of the window, descending the wall before disappearing under the back door. They made him think of a little stream of caviar. This intrusion greatly annoyed him. He opened the window and leaned out to see where they were coming from. Like a fearless and disciplined assault force, they were ascending from all the way down in the courtyard. They had apparently spurned the apartment below his, and the idea that they had gone straight for his floor was exasperating. He stuck a bit of newspaper into the corner of the window to block their route. They gradually entered by shifting to the left, not without difficulty, but successfully nevertheless. Quentin didn't have any insecticide in the house, and preferred to postpone combat until later, once he had procured the appropriate weaponry.

His morning was off to a bad start, his outlook bleak. Since the day Ghazi had borrowed that money, he and his posse seemed to have vanished. Almost in spite of himself, their disappearance was always somewhere on Quentin's mind. Several times a day, he caught himself trying to imagine why the little gang had abandoned a routine that he had thought immutable. Without them, the café seemed empty. The only sounds were the clicking at tric-trac tables and, through open windows, the banging of hammers, as if the whole alley were beating on gongs. The proprietor, worn out and puffy, would budge only to open or close the cash register drawer. Fixing his eyes on some distant horizon, he stared out onto the high seas of his personal reverie. The customers present, regulars for the most part (among whom Quentin could now be included) were unworthy of his attention.

Quentin lingered a bit longer than usual, then finally left for home, concluding that, on balance, the local beer wasn't as good as it had first seemed.

He often wondered what those boys could be doing with themselves during the day. None had a job that he knew of. Their families were poor, but they were always well-dressed and went to the café every evening. What kind of future was there for someone like Ghazi, too proud to do menial work but lacking any particular skills? Did he even know how to drive? Mercedes! What nerve!

That's when he got the idea of English lessons.

Why couldn't he get a job as chauffeur for some expatriates, after all? There were lots of embassies in Tahas. They were often looking for drivers. He was neat and well-groomed. If he knew a little English, they would take him for sure. He could give the kid two lessons a week, and in a few months, Ghazi would know enough to start a serious job search. Three lessons a week. Better that than hanging around the city and getting involved in who knows what kind of nasty business. It wasn't hard to see that they were all more or less delinquents, and that Ghazi was running the show. Maybe by giving him lessons, they could become friends, and Quentin might influence him, open up his horizons.

He went right over to the International Bookstore to purchase a how-to-learn-English book. He walked right past the historical shelves without so much as a glance, for a recent visit to the Archeological Institute had put a chill on his yearning for such erudition. He had been greeted by a rather attractive and elegant middle-aged woman seated at a little desk in the lobby. She asked him for his card, and he said he had come that morning to become a member. "Of course," she replied, taking out an application form, "and what is the topic of your dissertation?" Her pen in mid-air, she waited. Quentin understood then and there that he would never get beyond the lobby, and that his dreams of scholarly asceticism were simply wishful thinking.

He brought home two different study methods, and sat down right away to figure out which would best suit his future student: Quentin's desire for erudition might go unfulfilled, but he would take a stab at pedagogy.

Another week went by before Ghazi and his friends reappeared on the scene. Although Quentin had been expecting them to show up any day, he was still startled to see them walk into the café in their usual order: first, the little gang, loud and disorderly, then, a few steps back, Ghazi, head arrogantly aloft, greeting no one. Going over and offering English classes to this kid wasn't going to be easy.

He waited until the following day to broach the issue. He called Ghazi over to his table and laid out the proposal: he had spoken about him to several people in a position to hire him as a chauffeur, and all had set the same requirement of a decent command of English. That's what he'd been wanting to tell him. Personally, he advised that he get himself enrolled right away in one of the language schools downtown. Ghazi seemed annoyed at the idea. All these complications just to get into the driver's seat were exasperating. Visibly irritated, he replied that he didn't have the means to pay for classes like that—it was true, they tended to be expensive, and were attended mostly by people from the Ring. Quentin was pleased with the strategy he'd devised, which seemed to be working as predicted.

He pretended to be thinking. Ghazi was playing with the

ashtray, in stubborn silence. The moment had come: unless Quentin himself, after all . . . He could help him improve his English . . . Two or three times a week, they could work out an arrangement . . . Ghazi could come to his place the next day, even, around four, how was that?

Leaving the question unanswered, Ghazi returned to his table, bringing the conversation to a close.

So Quentin was a little surprised when, the following day, at four o'clock sharp, the doorbell rang.

Ghazi had brought a pen and a school notebook decorated with a childlike pattern of bear cubs alternating with dolls and blocks marked with bright letters of the alphabet.

They got started immediately. The young man didn't know much. He mumbled each word reluctantly and didn't like having his mistakes corrected. Here was a difficult pupil. He would often sit in silence rather than answer questions. Quentin waited patiently. Under the tan skin of the boy's neck, he could see the pulsing of a vein as it plunged into the open collar of his checked shirt. Intimidated now, he was starting to lose faith in his aptitude for teaching English.

For the second lesson, Ghazi was a half hour late, and over an hour for the third. He was becoming increasingly resistant. There was to be no fourth lesson, to Quentin's huge relief. And thus his teaching career came to a close, and with it his interest, ephemeral but sincere, in pedagogy.

His victory over the ants was short-lived. He had sown panic in their ranks with his bug spray, and for two days, the river of ants was dry. But by the third day, the column had formed once again. Discouraged, he gave up the fight, and resigned himself to looking on grimly as they paraded through his kitchen.

It was the same day he read a distressing news item in the Tahas Gazette. The article was entitled "Not Your Everyday Suicide":

> *This past Wednesday, M.Y., an American resident, employed as a photographer, took his own life in a startlingly unusual manner. He immersed himself in a vat of water set on a gas stove with all three burners lit. The lid of the vat, which allowed only his head to emerge, was padlocked from the inside. Neighbors alarmed by the screaming called the police, but they were unable save M.Y., who died while the rescue team was attempting to free him.*

The vision of this boiled man, whom Quentin believed he had once met back in his days as a new arrival, haunted him for some time to come. Rosemonde Goult's riff on the topic ("Ugh! Talk about beef stew!") was enough to put him off the taste of meat for a while.

Things weren't going so well, to say the least. The English class incident had left an unpleasant memory, and Quentin didn't like to think about it. Whenever he did, he experienced a peculiar sense of shame. And yet, he'd had nothing but good intentions.

His neighbors still wouldn't say hello in the stairwell, and averted their eyes whenever they crossed his path, so that he began to wonder whether he hadn't made a mistake leaving the Ring.

One morning, he found his car relieved of its side mirrors and hubcaps. Someone had already stolen his windshield wipers a few days before. There was no proof of hostile intent, of course. Such annoyances happen everywhere. He was nonetheless suspicious of his neighbors, and began to look more closely at the spare parts for sale in the alley.

He was thinking more and more about Europe now, which suddenly appeared irresistibly appealing. He forgot the rain, the gloom, the boredom of Sunday afternoons. In Tahas, everything felt harsh and hostile now. Deluded by its absence, his heart grew fonder of what he imagined as a friendly, gentle Europe.

It was at this point that he made the abrupt decision to leave. "Made" wasn't really the right verb, however, for the idea had found its way to him all by itself. Starting out subliminally, it had progressed each day, feeding on his many setbacks, and one morning the notion emerged fully formed, like those flowers that grow and bloom overnight. When Nina had asked him a few weeks earlier whether he was thinking about staying on in Tahas much longer, he had been unable to reply. He knew now that he had little to gain from prolonging his stay. His one-year contract was about to expire, as it happened. He would go see the Consul and declare his intention not to renew. He was under no obligation.

He was in such a hurry to leave that he wanted to start getting rid of the things that bound him to Tahas right away. He set about putting his house in order and began sorting, tidying, frenetically tossing out nearly everything in his path. After two hours, he realized he was still wavering over a number of miscellaneous items. It was hot and he felt all sticky with sweat. He would come back to his tidying later on, happy to know that he would not be spending another summer in this country.

He could hardly wait to speak with the Consul. He felt that his departure for Europe would remain uncertain until he had been officially released from his job. The rest—selling the car, dispatching his belongings—was a matter of secondary importance that he would handle later.

People were saying that the heat had come back too early for the season. Stepping outside, Quentin experienced a sudden rush of sensations that recalled the earlier part of his stay, one year ago. It was the same unwholesome air, the same dull light. A mustard-colored sun stuck to the leaden sky, looking motionless and ashamed, as if pilloried.

Once at the consulate, he learned of Jeanne Gaudin's death. A solemn-faced Rosemonde Goult announced it to him with an I-told-you-so attitude that made him want to slap her. Paul wouldn't be coming back for another month, and Quentin figured that they were liable to miss seeing each other by just a few days. In a cowardly way, he felt greatly relieved, for he had always dreaded encounters with people in mourning.

He was about to request an audience with the Consul when the phone rang. By coincidence, it was the Consul, and he happened to want a word with Quentin, all rather astonishing, given that Quentin had had no dealings with him since that very early encounter when he was first hired.

As he climbed the stairs, he mused over this coincidence—a kind of telepathy, perhaps?—and entered the Consul's office with a smile, ready to inform him that he would soon be parting company with his team of subalterns.

Things didn't turn out quite the way he had imagined, though they led to the same end result.

There was nothing about the Consul's person that was in any way striking, and Quentin thought that if he had crossed paths with him in the street, he wouldn't have recognized him. The man was speaking softly, politely, but seemed uncomfortable. He was probably the shy type. Quentin then made an effort to stop musing and to focus on what was being said, and what he heard made his ears blush: he was being let go, dismissed, in a word. Sacked! That would explain the discomfort he had noted in the Consul's expression. His contract would not be renewed. They were clearly holding something against him, though the reasons for this were kept vague. In short, Quentin wasn't up to the job here, and they wished him the best of luck in the future.

He descended the stairs in a wholly different frame of mind from the one he'd enjoyed on his way up only minutes before. He had wanted to announce his departure, but the Consul had beat him to the punch. They'd robbed him of his exit. He should have had the chance to explain that he himself, coincidentally, was just about to resign, but they would have found that childish, a spiteful reaction to the humiliation of dismissal. He would have appeared pathetic. Well, at least the work issue had been settled once and for all. In three weeks or so he would leave this job that he'd never really liked in the first place. He would then allow himself another few days in Tahas, maybe a week, after which he would leave the country behind, with few regrets.

There remained the problem of the car, which he would have to sell. He'd have to place some ads, but didn't really know how to go about it. People would want to see it, go for a test drive.

There would be phone calls, appointments, haggling. He could tell already that this fussing over the car was going to ruin his last weeks.

He raised the issue with Ghazi, in passing, just for something to talk about, since apart from cars, nothing else interested him.

"Give it to me."

Quentin wondered whether he'd heard correctly, and the other repeated:

"Give it to me, I could drive it as a taxi."

And he added:

"Sell it or don't sell it, you don't care much, right?"

Who in the world did this guy think he was? Quentin thought it better not to answer at all.

After their escapade, as yet unexplained, the group of boys were back at the Café du Port every evening, just as before. Quentin was happy to see them again. He found their presence oddly pleasant and reassuring, most likely for the simple reason that it had gradually taken on the patina of habit.

In practice, he had grown no closer to the little group, and there were often times when he would spend an entire evening without any of them, not even Ghazi, so much as looking his way. And yet, he sensed on several occasions that he was the subject of their conversation. Whenever that happened, he felt the force of that steely, young male gaze, and he would send back a vaguely apologetic smile, generic enough that it might well have been addressed to the customers at the next table.

They would always leave at more or less the same time. In general, it was Ghazi who gave the signal for departure, after looking at his watch—an impressive gold watch with multiple dials, which could give rise to all sorts of conjecture. Quentin would stay late, long after the boys had left the premises, because it was cooler there beneath the rotating fan blades that beat like giant insect wings, cooler in any case than his apartment, where the heat kept him awake well into the night.

In order to go serve his young customers, the proprietor left the helm momentarily to his second in command, an ageless man who was attempting to rectify his baldness with a huge moustache. Ordinarily, only his shining pate could be seen behind the counter where he was generally seated, constantly drinking tea from tiny cups. As soon as he saw the Ghazi gang enter, the proprietor called him over and yielded his place behind the till. These were the only times one could get a look at something other than the ivory white top of his head. He took money, gave back change, impassive and mute, his darkened silhouette set off sharply by the harshly lit white ceramic tiles that made this part of the café look like a bath house.

As the days went by, the name of the café lost its salty charm for Quentin, and only on rare occasions did it still conjure up a maritime horizon, or water lapping under a dock with little kissing sounds. But his seafaring dreams had been returning, lately, now that he had set a date for his departure. He knew he'd be flying back to Europe (he already had his ticket in a drawer at home), but whenever he thought of his imminent return, his imagination persisted in portraying a large white boat, like a giant swan. He wished he could sail off aboard some majestic ship to leave this country that he had not loved. Such a solemn departure should make his leaving somehow more definitive, irrevocable. But in airports swarming with departing planes, how could one dream of those grand leave-takings that used to split a life in two, when the aircraft roaring down the runway would be back the next day?

He would so much have preferred imagining himself standing on the stern, leaning against the railing as, one last time, the image of Tahas struggled to leave some imprint on his memory, before disappearing altogether into the ship's foamy wake. Then, as the pitch and roll caused him to stagger, the ship having now entered the high seas, he would make his way forward to the prow, his eyes now fixed on the purple horizon and, farther away still, toward the long, open-armed seawalls of some bustling Italian port.

Everywhere, clocks were keeping time, calendars displayed the succession of days, but for Quentin, time as he experienced it seemed somehow beyond standard chronology during these last weeks. Ever since his brief interview with the Consul, he had been afloat in an entirely subjective interval quite apart from general time, as if an interior water clock were counting out the hours more quickly. His days seemed to be tumbling down a slope, in constant acceleration, hurtling him toward his departure. As if time itself were collapsing beneath his feet.

At first, he had been reluctant to begin sorting through his things, deliberating at length before parting with this or that object, wondering what he ought to do with his wicker table and chairs. But it wasn't long before such matters lost all importance. As the departure date drew nearer, the fate of these worthless pieces of furniture mattered little to him anymore, and he simply left them where they were.

Likewise, he quite naturally came to lose interest in what would become of his car.

He was having trouble selling it, which was surprising, as it was a nice little car that would probably keep running for quite a while. But every time he found a potential buyer, something would always go wrong: one didn't show for the appointment, the other changed his mind, and still another demanded that he have the door repaired, but it was too late for that now.

One morning, he woke up wondering what had annoyed him so much about the idea of giving his car away to Ghazi. It was the perfect solution, wasn't it? He would be rid of the car for good, and would be performing an act of charity in the process. Two birds with one stone: he would satisfy both his laziness and his desire to be generous. He could already picture Ghazi settling down, earning an honest living as taxi driver. In a little while, he would marry a girl from the neighborhood, and disappear from the Café du Port. He'd put on a little weight. On Sundays, he would take his kids for a boat ride on the River Ovir. He could even pay for his brother Makki's English lessons.

As if on purpose, Ghazi failed to show up at the café that day. His friends were there as usual, but he never arrived. All day long, Quentin had thrilled at the thought of announcing his news. He stayed until closing time, for nothing.

The next evening, Ghazi did appear. There was a bloody slash across his cheek, and another gash above an eyebrow. Quentin pictured brawls, ambushes in dark basements, midnight clashes in vacant lots, settling old scores with switchblades, and the image of the family man on a Sunday outing, winking at his darlings as he rowed along the Ovir, was abruptly dispelled. He saw in that slashed cheek the disturbing symbol of a dangerous, incomprehensible life lived in zones that would remain unknowable to him, closed off. There was no place for Quentin in Ghazi's thoughts, he would never play any role in his life. The kid was violent and unscrupulous. He would never be a taxi driver. He was one of those people who fight, steal, and extort. It would be naïve, Quentin would be deluding himself, to imagine otherwise.

In his black shirt with rolled-up sleeves, Ghazi looked more swarthy than usual, and Quentin suddenly understood that he had been waiting all day for this moment, for Ghazi's entrance into the Café du Port.

The very next day, they went together to various bureaus to handle the paperwork. Such matters were always rather complicated, and could take all day. As it was his last week on the job, Quentin had no qualms about skipping out on the consulate for a few hours.

They went from one bureau to the next, carrying bundles of paper that grew ever thicker as the morning progressed. Hardly a word was exchanged between them. Finally, they had a long wait in a courtyard to get the final document stamped. The sun was starting to beat down, shadows getting shorter.

Quentin slipped away to buy cigarettes; when he got back, he found Ghazi absorbed in the contemplation of something moving on the ground, but which was too far away for him to make out. He approached quietly, trying instinctively not to attract the kid's attention, and he saw a little mouse near Ghazi's foot. The young man moved the tip of his shoe a bit, and the mouse fled into a corner of the courtyard and curled up, terrified. Then Ghazi moved stealthily forward, a bundle of papers in each hand, which he held like two dustpans to prevent the rodent from getting away. Quentin could no longer see the mouse, which was now eclipsed by Ghazi. Then, abruptly, the kid straightened up and pressed his foot into the base of the wall, applying his full weight. After what seemed forever, Quentin saw him pivot his foot furiously, as if he wanted to drive something into the ground, that movement one makes to fully extinguish a cigarette butt.

Two days later, Ghazi was the legal owner of a dark red car in which he could now be seen driving around the city, tires squealing, driving far too fast, with that arrogant look of his.

Quentin took leave of his coworkers in complete and mutual indifference. Paul was still absent, and was scheduled to get back a couple days later, but Quentin had already made up his mind not to seek him out again. It felt as if he had been gone for months. Quentin even had trouble remembering what he looked like. His sole point of reference was what he recalled as that goatlike look about him, so that now, all he could see when he tried to think of Paul was a caricature of a man with a goat's head. Paul's recent loss, and the misunderstanding that had marked their last exchange, made Quentin all the more reluctant to get back in touch. And what good was it, anyway, since he would be leaving in a week's time.

The send-off was tepid. The secretaries felt compelled, however, to do as they always did on such occasions, and got everyone together in their office around a bottle of local bubbly, which they drank lukewarm from plastic cups. Agnes had bought a chocolate cake, which no one could finish once they'd realized that the icing had gone bad. Quentin's successor was already there, and spoke to him in such a commiserating tone that he wondered whether the new arrival had mistaken him for his recently widowed colleague.

He walked out of the consulate for the last time, his mind oddly vacant. He walked a little bit along the Ring. It wasn't too hot out, almost pleasant, in fact. A little breeze rustled the already desiccated leaves of the hedges behind the gates. It occurred to him suddenly that he never did get back to Azga, and that he probably never would. Temperatures there must be very mild now. He'd always thought he and Clara would meet up there again one day, but then she left the country, and he never heard from her again. Which was a shame. In Garazdar, though, it was no doubt already too hot. And anyway, he wasn't about to set off on any trips, now that he had only five more days to spend in the country. It was odd, but the roar of time had ceased to resound in his ears, and in the resulting silence, the emptiness of these last days was almost dizzying. Endless and out of all proportion, they seemed to enclose a lifetime all their own.

There were few taxis, and all these were full and sped past him. A dark red car, a Japanese model, made his heart race. But it was a woman with a big head of black hair, and he brought his arm back down to his side. Eyes strained from looking out for the yellow crest of an available taxi, he was finally resigned to walking back to his apartment. It was quite a distance, but he was in no hurry and wasn't particularly tired. There was so little time that he suddenly had all the time in the world. He pondered this paradox for a moment, then forgot it as he descended the metal stairs that led to the Low Road. He walked by his old apartment building: he could picture how it looked at Ring level, the entrance with its pretentious, unsightly columns, and the five floors above, the fourth of which he occupied a long, long time ago.

The level where he now stood was where all the caretakers of these upscale buildings lived. Their doors gave onto the Low Road. They had access to the rest of the building by means of a stairway that, seen from up there, looked as if it plunged into an abyss. Behind the bars, painted bright blue, nothing was visible. Seen from outside, these dwellings looked like nothing but black holes, and brought to mind the sooty walls of caves inhabited by tribes of troglodytes. He recognized the caretaker's daughter seated like a good little girl on the cistern of a junked toilet flusher. She was playing with little stones, distractedly, while allowing her sweet Down syndrome smile to wander over passersby. She had a big egg stain on her checkered smock. Without knowing why, Quentin felt uncomfortable and looked the other way. He didn't feel like running into the little girl's father, and picked up his pace.

He was annoyed to wake up and find it was his usual hour to get up. On this, his first day devoid of any obligation, he had hoped to sleep in, but the heat, of course, had roused him. The sheets stuck to his damp extremities, and a mosquito was humming in his ear.

He got up and wanted to shower, but there wasn't enough water pressure. To wash, he had to patiently collect water in the sink from a tentative trickle that kept threatening to dry up altogether.

It was too hot to nurture any hope of accomplishing anything before evening, or at least until late afternoon when the sun wasn't so high. All Quentin could do was idle the day away, and the thought that he'd have to get through four more days of this before his departure depressed him terribly.

He checked the date on his plane ticket one more time, and put some papers in order. That kept him busy for a few minutes. After which he lay back on his still unmade bed and stared at two flies frolicking on the wall, and then the wall itself, once they had finished. He wondered whatever could have possessed him to wait these extra five days before leaving for Europe. Thinking through it, he found his own motivations completely mystifying. But it was too late to undo his mistake. He would manage to get through this stretch one way or another.

The previous day, he had made up his mind not to return to the Café du Port. Ever since he'd given Ghazi the car, he hadn't heard a word from him, and now had begun to detest him. It irked him that Ghazi hadn't even thanked him for the gift. Quentin hated him for being so different, so arrogant, for so often pretending not to see him, and finally, he hated him for being so ever-present on his mind these last few weeks. And so, to punish Ghazi, he told himself he would not be going back to the Café du Port. He realized now that he had been wrong to give Ghazi the car. It was nothing but a toy for him. He cruised around the neighborhood showing off to his friends, like kids doing wheelies in a parking lot. And Quentin hated Ghazi all the more for how long it had taken to come to this conclusion.

The heat was unbearable in the apartment, and Quentin went back to the Café du Port and sat at his customary table. He spent the afternoon in a daze, his eyes lost somewhere above the horizon of the bar, his hair stirred by the prevailing winds of a large floor fan.

By evening, he was still there, no longer drinking but just sitting, waiting for the urge to get up and leave. The group of boys came in and took their usual places at the other end of the room and asked to be brought sets of tric-trac. Quentin paid them no attention, gratified at how indifferent he now felt. He would have been foolish not to come and take advantage of the pleasant coolness of the well-ventilated café.

Someone was approaching his table. He raised his head: Ghazi stood before him and said something he didn't understand. Then the young man took a seat and kept talking. He wasn't easy to understand. He'd never learn English, that much was certain. But by paying close attention, Quentin managed to get the gist, and what he heard surprised him, for this Ghazi, who rarely even said hello, was now suddenly taking the initiative. And since he had nothing else of interest to do these final days in Tahas, Quentin was quick to accept the proposal.

The tomb was located a short distance outside the city and, according to what Quentin was able to grasp, it was not well-known to tourists and was very beautiful (it was probably one of those many tombs adorned with frescos that could be found in the region). They would go the next day, right around sunset to avoid the heat of the day (and Quentin was to bring a flashlight). They would meet up there, because Ghazi would be busy beforehand. As the kid's directions got more and more vague, Quentin handed him a pen and a bit of paper he chanced to find in his pocket (some official stationery, a remnant of his brief consular career) and Ghazi drew him a map. It wasn't as complicated as all that.

Then Quentin ordered a couple of beers, which they drank in silence, having nothing more to say to one another now that the topographical details had been issued and received.

Quentin went back home right afterward, with the feeling that time had been set in motion once again, and slept quite well that night.

When he dropped him off, the taxi driver made a vague arm motion in the direction of the mound, having repeated several times that this was indeed the place, but a bit farther on, over and behind. He then took off without waiting, without even counting the money he'd been given. He'd simply stuffed it into a tin that must have once contained candy, and drove off, almost angrily.

This little mound was part of the cemetery, and there were tombs everywhere, scattered randomly, it would appear. The easiest way would have been to walk around it, but there were so few points of elevation in Tahas that Quentin could not resist the urge to climb to the top. There might even be an interesting view.

His shoes dug into the sandy slope. His foot slipped back a few centimeters with each step, making him feel as if he were floundering, not getting anywhere. Little white bones kept emerging here and there in the grayish soil. There were so many that it was becoming rather alarming, until he took a closer look and realized they were nothing but ordinary stones.

When he got to the top, his shoes were full of sand. There was no use emptying them, since they'd only fill again on the way down. At the bottom of the mound, he located the column that Ghazi had marked with an X on the map.

In the distance, he could make out some farmland that the combination of remoteness and the fading light tinted a slate gray. He had never ventured out there. Of Tahas, he knew only the city and the desert, and disliked both.

He could see the Ovir quite distinctly from here. It flowed from deep in the hinterland, far beyond the borders of this country. It cut through the city, splitting it in half, then made its way north to finally flow into the sea, some two hundred kilometers from Tahas. If he squinted, Quentin thought he could make out the dark line of a new bridge downstream, over where the sluices were located. Out past that, everything faded into the mist.

The sun was setting quickly, tarnished by the city's exhalations. It would soon be nothing but a dull ember glowing among the ashes. Two large crows were fighting over something down below.

Quentin took a last look at the map to check which path to take, then descended the mound, heels first, almost at a run. Once at the column, he was supposed to take the path to the left, which continued downhill a bit, and there, in a hollow, he'd find the tomb.

Ghazi wasn't there. Quentin had arrived first, then. He sat down on a large rock and waited. To pass the time, he fiddled with his flashlight, making it blink red, then white, orange, and green. It probably wasn't so smart to be using up the battery like that. He stopped. There wasn't a whole lot to look at. The place where he sat was below the path, so that he could no longer even see the mound he'd climbed only moments before. It was surprising to discover this relatively uneven terrain where it had earlier appeared perfectly flat.

Birds crisscrossed above, crying out as they do before a storm. Clouds of black smoke billowed against the bleached sky. They hovered, in search of a breeze to carry them off, and having found one, slipped slowly sideways, more and more dispersed, evanescent, and finally gone altogether, while others appeared in their place. A moment ago, from atop the mound, Quentin had seen that the smoke was coming from small edifices that were probably brick kilns. Sooty and smoking, one might have mistaken them for the burned-out houses of a village having weathered some disaster. Behind the enclosures of blackened stone, he'd seen the glow of flames.

A dog was barking somewhere far off to the right and others replied from over on the left. As he listened, Quentin sensed that the barking was getting closer. The wife of the Dutch Consul—or Danish, he couldn't recall—had died of rabies a few weeks earlier: a dog seeking shade under her car was roused when she opened the door. She had been vaccinated, but the expiration date on the medicine had probably passed, and she died. Things like that happen. Judging from the commotion they were making, there had to be at least a half dozen dogs now, and they were still getting closer. In an attempt to evaluate how many there were and how far away, Quentin listened intently, anxiously, holding his breath, just as he had done as a boy, to measure how close lightning had struck by counting the seconds before the thunder.

It suddenly dawned on him how absurd it was to be sitting in this ditch on the edge of a cemetery, and he decided to head back. Anyway, it was starting to get dark. He had been there almost an hour, like a languishing Romeo waiting in vain for his lady. And besides, he was afraid of the dogs. He heaved a great sigh, looked conspicuously at his watch to signal he'd run out of patience, and got up.

It was then they swooped down on him, as if his movement had been their signal to attack. They were all over him, screaming like a murder of crows, and Quentin was thrown to the ground.

Oddly enough, his fear seemed to vanish all at once. What was happening was so new, so abrupt, that he no longer felt afraid. Face down on the ground, he was mainly concerned with the sandy soil that had got into his mouth, and he attempted to spit it out in short bursts. He could hear their laughter from above, then several times heard a strange cry, inappropriate, unseemly—why would they be making a noise like that?

Now he was on his back, and he saw a club coming down on him while others were holding his arms and legs. He then understood that the person crying out was none other than himself, and that he would continue crying out unabated, unable to stop. (Hearing this cry, an elderly lady writing her memoirs by lamplight perhaps raised her head and listened more closely. But no, she must have imagined it; there was no one like that around these parts.) Quentin had just enough time to see the dials on the watch. Why in the world wear a watch like that for this sort of operation, he was surely going to break it, such an expensive watch . . . Just then, a flash of pain streaked through his head.

He could open only one eye, his right. His left eyelid was swollen shut, and only with enormous effort could he manage to see a blurry slit of light through it. He fell back into unconsciousness several times, in and out of sleep and waking.

Behind his pillow, there were cream-colored metal bars that he didn't recognize. The first move he made to get up produced a stabbing pain to the head that reminded him of his assailants' blows. He cautiously turned his head and saw he was surrounded by dull yellow walls. Dust motes played in a ray of sunlight coming through a tall, grated window. The bed next to his was empty.

He panicked at the idea that he might be in prison, but he soon saw that the room he was in opened onto a second, smaller one, and there, judging from the ambient daylight, a door certainly led outside. It couldn't be a prison, then. An infirmary, perhaps. Someone was typing in the next room. He could also hear two men conversing and laughing loudly, and farther on, a buzzing of voices, muffled as if from behind a wall.

Then, he fell back to sleep.

In his dream, someone was asking him something insistently, but he could not reply because he didn't have the right to speak, while the other didn't understand this and kept asking, asking . . .

When he woke up, Paul Gaudin was sitting next to his bed and was saying something. Quentin didn't immediately recognize the face, which seemed to belong to a very distant past. He couldn't figure out what Paul was doing in this place and why he was speaking so softly, the way one talks to someone who is seriously ill. He was saying that Quentin had been lucky, but he really couldn't see why he should be saying that.

Someone brought them some tea. Quentin was having trouble with the sleeves of his borrowed garment (a khaki shirt, much too big for him). He asked what had become of his clothes, his keys, his wallet, and Paul resumed his explanation to say that he had been found unconscious, his clothes torn to shreds, near the entrance to the eastern cemetery; that his assailants had robbed him, since nothing was found except the map of the location drawn, fortunately, on official stationery, thanks to which the police had contacted the consulate; that some kid had followed him and witnessed the whole scene and called his mother, who immediately called the police; by the time they arrived, the assailants—young men, six or seven of them—had got away; that they would be coming to question him in an effort to identify the attackers; that it was the kid who found the keys, in the sand; and that a doctor would be coming to examine him. Quentin really was very lucky.

The air in the room was thick with the sickening odor of sweat and stale bread. Paul explained further that they were presently at the eastern-sector police station and that there were detainees in the next room. When he heard this, Quentin looked upset.

"I didn't mean you, of course not, you're free. What did you think?"

But the police did have to search for the assailants, or at least pretend to.

Get out of here, get back home . . . Never have to deal with these people ever again.

A policeman entered the room without any form of greeting. He was huge in his khaki uniform. It occurred to Quentin that the shirt he'd been given might well belong to this fellow, and the idea of any resemblance between this individual and himself, even if it was only an article of clothing, deeply revolted him. He wished that Paul could have stayed by his bedside, but that wasn't allowed.

The policeman, speaking in English, asked him his name, surname, profession, home address; and why he had he been at that location; and what was the tomb marked on the map; and who were the assailants. Quentin didn't know. What did he mean, he didn't know? He had arranged to meet them there, hadn't he? Really, he had nothing to say? He shrugged his shoulders. All right, then. If that was his idea of a good time, meeting up with some thugs to stare at the moon and get himself beat to a pulp, that was his business—to each his own, I guess! And he exited, in a burst of laughter. Quentin heard him telling the story—what other story would he be telling—to a couple of his colleagues, who responded with bawdy snickers.

The doctor was built like a greyhound, and like the policeman, failed to reciprocate Quentin's greeting. Perhaps that was one of the rules enforced at police stations. He removed the bandages, disinfected the wounds, replaced the bandages with smaller ones, and declared that he would be fine, it was nothing serious. Nowhere in his voice or manner was there anything resembling compassion, but rather a sternness, a disapproval—disgust, even, as if he had been obliged to care for a particularly repulsive criminal, bound by his profession alone to examine him.

Quentin rested a few hours more, relieved to know that he would be left alone from here on, and that he could go home.

Toward evening, Paul came to get him. He brought Quentin some clothes, since his own had been torn to shreds (indeed, he had been found half-naked, with only his shoes untouched).

They said nothing during the drive home. Quentin racked his brain for anything he could possibly say to thank Paul. He should also have said something about his wife, presented his condolences. There were conventions for such things, but the words stuck in his throat.

When they got to his neighborhood, Quentin had to tell Paul the way and it was only this that finally broke the silence.

As they entered his building, Quentin felt ashamed of the filthy lobby, the four flights of poorly lit stairs they had to climb, the graffiti-smeared walls, whose filth you could scrape off with a knife. Quentin's legs still ached, so he went slowly, ahead of Paul, up the stairs, which were either slick or sticky, depending on what had been spilled there most recently. Quentin stopped before tackling the last flight and glanced upward.

On his door was a white spot that recalled the body of a large dead bird, wings spread and nailed to the wood. The violence that emanated from this thing crucified to his door startled him, and he felt his knees shaking as he climbed the final steps: it was Nina's tutu, which they had nailed to the door by way of a message. Several heavy nails had been pounded furiously through the satin and tulle—as if to purge the effigy of all that was beautiful, noble, fine.

His door wasn't closed. They had forced their way in and torn the place apart: they had sliced the drapes, disemboweled the pillows, emptied the closets, and painted obscene pictures all over the walls (in which Quentin's name featured so clearly that, despite the awkward handwriting, there would be no mistaking it).

He swallowed hard. Paul remained silent at his side. The drawers were all wide open and empty. They had taken his money, his passport, his plane ticket. He searched everywhere in the desperate hope of finding the latter two items, which they might have hidden in some peculiar spot, just for laughs.

Then Paul asked him how much he would be needing. He

would lend him the money for his ticket and expenses. And if he didn't feel like returning to the consulate, he would handle the paperwork for getting a new passport. And if he'd rather not spend the night here, he was welcome to stay with him until his departure.

And Quentin heard himself saying no thank you, that he wouldn't be needing anything, that he still had his checks and money in his bank account, since he had sold his car, that he'd just as soon stay at his own place, and finally, that he wanted to be left alone.

Paul said nothing at first, then simply replied that it was up to him, and he headed for the door.

"You should probably take this down," he said, pointing to the tutu, then made his way down through the darkness of the stairwell.

Dumbstruck, Quentin stood staring at the gaping door through which the only man in the world who still wished him well had just exited. When he tried to close it, he saw that the lock had been torn away. The door, as though consumed with ill will, hung open. He ended up shoving a table against it, relieved to be sheltered from the hostile looks that he felt seeping out of the stairwell.

A fly landed on his face, as they always did at that hour, and woke him up. The sun poured in through the lacerated curtains. He must have had nightmares: he'd woken up once or twice during the night, beset by some childhood fear, but he couldn't remember what he had dreamed.

The sight of the room sickened him, but before tackling the job of making some order out of the mess, he had to leave the apartment, walk a little, get some air.

Everything was still intact in the bathroom: they hadn't broken the faucets, or unscrewed the showerhead, or smeared excrement on the walls; nor had they written anything horrible on the mirror with his shaving cream. Taking these positive signs for what they were worth, Quentin showered and shaved with care. The swelling on his eye had gone down some. He chose to remove the bandage on his forehead, figuring that the wound would be less noticeable than a big square of white gauze. The clothes Paul had brought him at the police station were a perfect fit.

He pulled the table away and went out, leaving the door wide open. That Nina's tutu was still nailed to the door made no difference to him anymore.

As he descended the stairs, his legs were still sore, though it felt more like his normal stiffness now, and he thought that a little exercise would do him some good. He still had a throbbing headache.

It was lovely outside. The day promised to be less stifling than the previous few, and the light breeze blowing through his hair seemed to bode well. His troubles appeared to be over, the worst was behind him. Perhaps he had been lucky after all. He would phone Paul, who would handle everything. He would be leaving soon, just a bit later than expected.

He wandered aimlessly. There weren't many people on the street yet. In this country, people tend to live at night in the summer. He soon found himself on an endless street lined with nothing but electrical supply shops behind filthy windows. His knee was starting to hurt. In the right-hand pocket of his trousers, his hand came upon two bills that Paul had either forgotten or had left there for him on purpose (which, now that he thought about it, was the most likely explanation). He crossed the street and entered a pharmacy. The pharmacist was old and nearly blind. Quentin's request—some aspirin, as it happened—left the man puzzled for a moment. With both hands trembling, he dug through a shoebox full of medications before coming up with a tube, which he had to hold a few centimeters from his eyes to check whether it was the one he was looking for. Quentin decided against asking him for a glass of water, and left. He chewed a couple of the tablets and resumed his walk.

The lone vehicle in this dismal street, a taxi, was waiting parked at the curb, an antiquated model, but its black body shone as though lacquered, and its chrome was gleaming. It seemed to be waiting for no one but him.

Quentin got in and, in a burst of inspiration, asked the driver to take him to a place he'd never been before, but that people said was quite pleasant, a place called the Ovir Gardens. A little north of Tahas, it was known for its riverbank cafés and restaurants.

The place was just as he'd heard, with shaded terraces right on the water and kiosks where they probably played music in the evenings. It was fairly deserted at this hour. Waiters were preparing tables, making the gravel crunch as they dragged chairs into place. Barefoot, trouser legs rolled up, a man was watering down the paths. Quentin could feel a rush of cool air smelling of chalk. Overhead, tall trees were waving their clusters of mauve flowers. He relished the thought that he would be getting back to Europe in time to enjoy all the charms of summer, to spend the evening sitting under the hundred-year-old trees of some country café, watching with delight the condensation forming on a carafe while the soundless night gathered beneath the branches. Then would come autumn, falling leaves, and bursting chestnuts.

He would have lunch there. His headache had almost completely disappeared now, and he felt the need to get some exercise. He went down toward the pontoon where one could rent little rowboats painted in red and blue. There was no one there yet, all the boats docked and docile, patiently awaiting customers. There were also pedal boats.

Quentin went over to the person in charge of rentals who sat crouched at the far end of the pontoon, spitting into the water, just to have something to do. As soon as Quentin set foot onto the unsteady boards, he felt transported. All the things he had been missing were suddenly granted to him as he heard the sound of his footsteps on the pontoon, the scraping of chains on the wooden hulls, the lapping of the water. All the excitement, the joy, the pleasure he had ever experienced during vacation trips or outings going all the way back to his childhood, all the old delights, the forgotten happiness, came surging back.

The man had him get into one of the boats, which he then unmoored and pushed gently away from the pontoon with the help of a pole. Quentin took the oars.

At first he noticed a little soreness in his arms, but that was soon gone. It felt good to row steadily, conscientiously. He was a student at an English boarding school and they had organized a big regatta for their end-of-year celebration. His skiff slid along the water like an eel. Order. Steadfastness. Discipline. He would be the winner.

He slowed down a bit, but continued to row steadily, taking care to synchronize his breathing.

He soon reached a red and white pole that marked the outer limit of where boats could safely go, and he rowed right past it, because it would have been a shame, wouldn't it, to have to turn back so soon. It was easier to row in the middle of the river because the current carried the boat along. The sun was getting higher, burning away the relative coolness of the morning. It occurred to him that he should be wearing a hat out on the water like this, in full sun. The light was dazzling. If he squinted, he could see the city of Tahas—at this distance, it seemed more compact. A cloud hung over it, like some dark ghost. On the horizon, he could see the billowing white smoke of the cement works. Here, though, the air was pure and one could really breathe.

Over his shoulder, he caught sight of the bridge, still a ways off downriver. He had plenty of time. In a little bit, he would have to get over to the banks, where there was hardly any current, and turn around before getting to the sluices.

He stopped rowing because his left arm was starting to cramp, and stretched out for a moment on the bottom of the boat. Gazing upward, he watched the fathomless blue flying by. He closed his eyes, and beneath the bloody veil of his eyelids danced bubbles of light, stars, wheels, spirals. One of his dreams suddenly came back to him. He had gone into a gray building that felt like a military barracks. There was an awful silence. Dust was suspended in the air, as if it dared not settle. An ageless woman was there, seated. She had always been there. He longed to ask her a question that had been tormenting him for a good while. He absolutely had to ask it, even though he already knew the answer because of a medallion she was wearing—a diamond-studded clover. The woman didn't answer right away. She was busy sewing together pieces of flesh-colored fabric. She then raised her head and said, "My poor boy, your parents died a long time ago. Look, this is all that's left of them," and she gestured wearily to the bits of fabric she was stitching. And he wept and wept.

He didn't feel like opening his eyes again. He tried to gauge the distance to the sluices, but couldn't. He was too weak or too drowsy to get up and look. He allowed himself another few minutes of rest; he would take up the oars in a little bit.

A while later, he realized that he had almost fallen asleep in the blazing sun. On second thought, he probably had dozed off for a few seconds, in fact. Now he really had to rouse himself, shake off this fatigue, and grab the oars.

But the sun was beating down so hard, and he was so weary. He had just enough time to make a mental note in Nina's little blue notebook:

Quentin Corbal, Tahas, July 199–

Then the current quickened, and he felt the first tug of the sluices, like a battering ram, slam the bottom of the boat.

Elisabeth Horem was born in Bourges, France, in 1955, and was educated in Paris, where she studied Arabic. She has traveled extensively, and spent many years in the Middle East with her husband, a Swiss diplomat.

Jane Kuntz has translated, among other titles, *Hotel Crystal* by Olivier Rolin, *Pigeon Post* by Dumitru Tsepeneag, and *Hoppla! 1 2 3* by Gérard Gavarry, all of which are available from Dalkey Archive Press.

SELECTED DALKEY ARCHIVE TITLES

Michal Ajvaz, *The Golden Age.*
The Other City.
Pierre Albert-Birot, *Grabinoulor.*
Yuz Aleshkovsky, *Kangaroo.*
Felipe Alfau, *Chromos.*
Locos.
Ivan Ângelo, *The Celebration.*
The Tower of Glass.
António Lobo Antunes, *Knowledge of Hell.*
The Splendor of Portugal.
Alain Arias-Misson, *Theatre of Incest.*
John Ashbery and James Schuyler, *A Nest of Ninnies.*
Robert Ashley, *Perfect Lives.*
Gabriela Avigur-Rotem, *Heatwave and Crazy Birds.*
Djuna Barnes, *Ladies Almanack.*
Ryder.
John Barth, *LETTERS.*
Sabbatical.
Donald Barthelme, *The King.*
Paradise.
Svetislav Basara, *Chinese Letter.*
Miquel Bauçà, *The Siege in the Room.*
René Belletto, *Dying.*
Marek Bieńczyk, *Transparency.*
Andrei Bitov, *Pushkin House.*
Andrej Blatnik, *You Do Understand.*
Louis Paul Boon, *Chapel Road.*
My Little War.
Summer in Termuren.
Roger Boylan, *Killoyle.*
Ignácio de Loyola Brandão, *Anonymous Celebrity.*
Zero.
Bonnie Bremser, *Troia: Mexican Memoirs.*
Christine Brooke-Rose, *Amalgamemnon.*
Brigid Brophy, *In Transit.*
Gerald L. Bruns, *Modern Poetry and the Idea of Language.*
Gabrielle Burton, *Heartbreak Hotel.*
Michel Butor, *Degrees.*
Mobile.
G. Cabrera Infante, *Infante's Inferno.*
Three Trapped Tigers.
Julieta Campos, *The Fear of Losing Eurydice.*
Anne Carson, *Eros the Bittersweet.*
Orly Castel-Bloom, *Dolly City.*
Louis-Ferdinand Céline, *Castle to Castle.*
Conversations with Professor Y.
London Bridge.
Normance.
North.
Rigadoon.
Marie Chaix, *The Laurels of Lake Constance.*
Hugo Charteris, *The Tide Is Right.*
Eric Chevillard, *Demolishing Nisard.*
Marc Cholodenko, *Mordechai Schamz.*
Joshua Cohen, *Witz.*
Emily Holmes Coleman, *The Shutter of Snow.*
Robert Coover, *A Night at the Movies.*
Stanley Crawford, *Log of the S.S. The Mrs Unguentine.*
Some Instructions to My Wife.
René Crevel, *Putting My Foot in It.*
Ralph Cusack, *Cadenza.*
Nicholas Delbanco, *The Count of Concord.*
Sherbrookes.
Nigel Dennis, *Cards of Identity.*
Peter Dimock, *A Short Rhetoric for Leaving the Family.*
Ariel Dorfman, *Konfidenz.*
Coleman Dowell, *Island People.*
Too Much Flesh and Jabez.
Arkadii Dragomoshchenko, *Dust.*
Rikki Ducornet, *The Complete Butcher's Tales.*
The Fountains of Neptune.
The Jade Cabinet.
Phosphor in Dreamland.
William Eastlake, *The Bamboo Bed.*
Castle Keep.
Lyric of the Circle Heart.
Jean Echenoz, *Chopin's Move.*
Stanley Elkin, *A Bad Man.*
Criers and Kibitzers, Kibitzers and Criers.
The Dick Gibson Show.
The Franchiser.
The Living End.
Mrs. Ted Bliss.
François Emmanuel, *Invitation to a Voyage.*
Salvador Espriu, *Ariadne in the Grotesque Labyrinth.*
Leslie A. Fiedler, *Love and Death in the American Novel.*
Juan Filloy, *Op Oloop.*
Andy Fitch, *Pop Poetics.*
Gustave Flaubert, *Bouvard and Pécuchet.*
Kass Fleisher, *Talking out of School.*
Ford Madox Ford, *The March of Literature.*
Jon Fosse, *Aliss at the Fire.*
Melancholy.
Max Frisch, *I'm Not Stiller.*
Man in the Holocene.
Carlos Fuentes, *Christopher Unborn.*
Distant Relations.
Terra Nostra.
Where the Air Is Clear.
Takehiko Fukunaga, *Flowers of Grass.*
William Gaddis, *J R.*
The Recognitions.
Janice Galloway, *Foreign Parts.*
The Trick Is to Keep Breathing.
William H. Gass, *Cartesian Sonata and Other Novellas.*
Finding a Form.
A Temple of Texts.
The Tunnel.
Willie Masters' Lonesome Wife.
Gérard Gavarry, *Hoppla! 1 2 3.*
Etienne Gilson, *The Arts of the Beautiful.*
Forms and Substances in the Arts.
C. S. Giscombe, *Giscome Road.*
Here.
Douglas Glover, *Bad News of the Heart.*
Witold Gombrowicz, *A Kind of Testament.*
Paulo Emílio Sales Gomes, *P's Three Women.*
Georgi Gospodinov, *Natural Novel.*
Juan Goytisolo, *Count Julian.*
Juan the Landless.
Makbara.
Marks of Identity.

SELECTED DALKEY ARCHIVE TITLES

Henry Green, *Back.*
Blindness.
Concluding.
Doting.
Nothing.
Jack Green, *Fire the Bastards!*
Jiří Gruša, *The Questionnaire.*
Mela Hartwig, *Am I a Redundant Human Being?*
John Hawkes, *The Passion Artist.*
Whistlejacket.
Elizabeth Heighway, ed., *Contemporary Georgian Fiction.*
Aleksandar Hemon, ed., *Best European Fiction.*
Aidan Higgins, *Balcony of Europe.*
Blind Man's Bluff
Bornholm Night-Ferry.
Flotsam and Jetsam.
Langrishe, Go Down.
Scenes from a Receding Past.
Keizo Hino, *Isle of Dreams.*
Kazushi Hosaka, *Plainsong.*
Aldous Huxley, *Antic Hay.*
Crome Yellow.
Point Counter Point.
Those Barren Leaves.
Time Must Have a Stop.
Naoyuki Ii, *The Shadow of a Blue Cat.*
Gert Jonke, *The Distant Sound.*
Geometric Regional Novel.
Homage to Czerny.
The System of Vienna.
Jacques Jouet, *Mountain R.*
Savage.
Upstaged.
Mieko Kanai, *The Word Book.*
Yoram Kaniuk, *Life on Sandpaper.*
Hugh Kenner, *Flaubert.*
Joyce and Beckett: The Stoic Comedians.
Joyce's Voices.
Danilo Kiš, *The Attic.*
Garden, Ashes.
The Lute and the Scars
Psalm 44.
A Tomb for Boris Davidovich.
Anita Konkka, *A Fool's Paradise.*
George Konrád, *The City Builder.*
Tadeusz Konwicki, *A Minor Apocalypse.*
The Polish Complex.
Menis Koumandareas, *Koula.*
Elaine Kraf, *The Princess of 72nd Street.*
Jim Krusoe, *Iceland.*
Ayşe Kulin, *Farewell: A Mansion in Occupied Istanbul.*
Emilio Lascano Tegui, *On Elegance While Sleeping.*
Eric Laurrent, *Do Not Touch.*
Violette Leduc, *La Bâtarde.*
Edouard Levé, *Autoportrait.*
Suicide.
Mario Levi, *Istanbul Was a Fairy Tale.*
Deborah Levy, *Billy and Girl.*
José Lezama Lima, *Paradiso.*
Rosa Liksom, *Dark Paradise.*
Osman Lins, *Avalovara.*
The Queen of the Prisons of Greece.
Alf Mac Lochlainn, *The Corpus in the Library.*
Out of Focus.
Ron Loewinsohn, *Magnetic Field(s).*
Mina Loy, *Stories and Essays of Mina Loy.*
D. Keith Mano, *Take Five.*
Micheline Aharonian Marcom, *The Mirror in the Well.*
Ben Marcus, *The Age of Wire and String.*
Wallace Markfield, *Teitlebaum's Window.*
To an Early Grave.
David Markson, *Reader's Block.*
Wittgenstein's Mistress.
Carole Maso, *AVA.*
Ladislav Matejka and Krystyna Pomorska, eds., *Readings in Russian Poetics: Formalist and Structuralist Views.*
Harry Mathews, *Cigarettes.*
The Conversions.
The Human Country: New and Collected Stories.
The Journalist.
My Life in CIA.
Singular Pleasures.
The Sinking of the Odradek Stadium.
Tlooth.
Joseph McElroy, *Night Soul and Other Stories.*
Abdelwahab Meddeb, *Talismano.*
Gerhard Meier, *Isle of the Dead.*
Herman Melville, *The Confidence-Man.*
Amanda Michalopoulou, *I'd Like.*
Steven Millhauser, *The Barnum Museum.*
In the Penny Arcade.
Ralph J. Mills, Jr., *Essays on Poetry.*
Momus, *The Book of Jokes.*
Christine Montalbetti, *The Origin of Man.*
Western.
Olive Moore, *Spleen.*
Nicholas Mosley, *Accident.*
Assassins.
Catastrophe Practice.
Experience and Religion.
A Garden of Trees.
Hopeful Monsters.
Imago Bird.
Impossible Object.
Inventing God.
Judith.
Look at the Dark.
Natalie Natalia.
Serpent.
Time at War.
Warren Motte, *Fables of the Novel: French Fiction since 1990.*
Fiction Now: The French Novel in the 21st Century.
Oulipo: A Primer of Potential Literature.
Gerald Murnane, *Barley Patch.*
Inland.
Yves Navarre, *Our Share of Time.*
Sweet Tooth.
Dorothy Nelson, *In Night's City.*
Tar and Feathers.
Eshkol Nevo, *Homesick.*
Wilfrido D. Nolledo, *But for the Lovers.*
Flann O'Brien, *At Swim-Two-Birds.*
The Best of Myles.
The Dalkey Archive.
The Hard Life.
The Poor Mouth.

SELECTED DALKEY ARCHIVE TITLES

The Third Policeman.
CLAUDE OLLIER, *The Mise-en-Scène.*
Wert and the Life Without End.
GIOVANNI ORELLI, *Walaschek's Dream.*
PATRIK OUŘEDNÍK, *Europeana.*
The Opportune Moment, 1855.
BORIS PAHOR, *Necropolis.*
FERNANDO DEL PASO, *News from the Empire.*
Palinuro of Mexico.
ROBERT PINGET, *The Inquisitory.*
Mahu or The Material.
Trio.
MANUEL PUIG, *Betrayed by Rita Hayworth.*
The Buenos Aires Affair.
Heartbreak Tango.
RAYMOND QUENEAU, *The Last Days.*
Odile.
Pierrot Mon Ami.
Saint Glinglin.
ANN QUIN, *Berg.*
Passages.
Three.
Tripticks.
ISHMAEL REED, *The Free-Lance Pallbearers.*
The Last Days of Louisiana Red.
Ishmael Reed: The Plays.
Juice!
Reckless Eyeballing.
The Terrible Threes.
The Terrible Twos.
Yellow Back Radio Broke-Down.
JASIA REICHARDT, *15 Journeys Warsaw to London.*
NOËLLE REVAZ, *With the Animals.*
JOÃO UBALDO RIBEIRO, *House of the Fortunate Buddhas.*
JEAN RICARDOU, *Place Names.*
RAINER MARIA RILKE, *The Notebooks of Malte Laurids Brigge.*
JULIÁN RÍOS, *The House of Ulysses.*
Larva: A Midsummer Night's Babel.
Poundemonium.
Procession of Shadows.
AUGUSTO ROA BASTOS, *I the Supreme.*
DANIËL ROBBERECHTS, *Arriving in Avignon.*
JEAN ROLIN, *The Explosion of the Radiator Hose.*
OLIVIER ROLIN, *Hotel Crystal.*
ALIX CLEO ROUBAUD, *Alix's Journal.*
JACQUES ROUBAUD, *The Form of a City Changes Faster, Alas, Than the Human Heart.*
The Great Fire of London.
Hortense in Exile.
Hortense Is Abducted.
The Loop.
Mathematics:
The Plurality of Worlds of Lewis.
The Princess Hoppy.
Some Thing Black.
RAYMOND ROUSSEL, *Impressions of Africa.*
VEDRANA RUDAN, *Night.*
STIG SÆTERBAKKEN, *Siamese.*
Self Control.
LYDIE SALVAYRE, *The Company of Ghosts.*
The Lecture.
The Power of Flies.
LUIS RAFAEL SÁNCHEZ, *Macho Camacho's Beat.*
SEVERO SARDUY, *Cobra & Maitreya.*
NATHALIE SARRAUTE, *Do You Hear Them?*
Martereau.
The Planetarium.
ARNO SCHMIDT, *Collected Novellas.*
Collected Stories.
Nobodaddy's Children.
Two Novels.
ASAF SCHURR, *Motti.*
GAIL SCOTT, *My Paris.*
DAMION SEARLS, *What We Were Doing and Where We Were Going.*
JUNE AKERS SEESE, *Is This What Other Women Feel Too?*
What Waiting Really Means.
BERNARD SHARE, *Inish.*
Transit.
VIKTOR SHKLOVSKY, *Bowstring.*
Knight's Move.
A Sentimental Journey: Memoirs 1917–1922.
Energy of Delusion: A Book on Plot.
Literature and Cinematography.
Theory of Prose.
Third Factory.
Zoo, or Letters Not about Love.
PIERRE SINIAC, *The Collaborators.*
KJERSTI A. SKOMSVOLD, *The Faster I Walk, the Smaller I Am.*
JOSEF ŠKVORECKÝ, *The Engineer of Human Souls.*
GILBERT SORRENTINO, *Aberration of Starlight.*
Blue Pastoral.
Crystal Vision.
Imaginative Qualities of Actual Things.
Mulligan Stew.
Pack of Lies.
Red the Fiend.
The Sky Changes.
Something Said.
Splendide-Hôtel.
Steelwork.
Under the Shadow.
W. M. SPACKMAN, *The Complete Fiction.*
ANDRZEJ STASIUK, *Dukla.*
Fado.
GERTRUDE STEIN, *The Making of Americans.*
A Novel of Thank You.
LARS SVENDSEN, *A Philosophy of Evil.*
PIOTR SZEWC, *Annihilation.*
GONÇALO M. TAVARES, *Jerusalem.*
Joseph Walser's Machine.
Learning to Pray in the Age of Technique.
LUCIAN DAN TEODOROVICI, *Our Circus Presents . . .*
NIKANOR TERATOLOGEN, *Assisted Living.*
STEFAN THEMERSON, *Hobson's Island.*
The Mystery of the Sardine.
Tom Harris.
TAEKO TOMIOKA, *Building Waves.*
JOHN TOOMEY, *Sleepwalker.*
JEAN-PHILIPPE TOUSSAINT, *The Bathroom.*
Camera.
Monsieur.
Reticence.
Running Away.
Self-Portrait Abroad.
Television.
The Truth about Marie.

SELECTED DALKEY ARCHIVE TITLES

Dumitru Tsepeneag, *Hotel Europa.*
The Necessary Marriage.
Pigeon Post.
Vain Art of the Fugue.
Esther Tusquets, *Stranded.*
Dubravka Ugresic, *Lend Me Your Character.*
Thank You for Not Reading.
Tor Ulven, *Replacement.*
Mati Unt, *Brecht at Night.*
Diary of a Blood Donor.
Things in the Night.
Álvaro Uribe and Olivia Sears, eds., *Best of Contemporary Mexican Fiction.*
Eloy Urroz, *Friction.*
The Obstacles.
Luisa Valenzuela, *Dark Desires and the Others.*
He Who Searches.
Paul Verhaeghen, *Omega Minor.*
Aglaja Veteranyi, *Why the Child Is Cooking in the Polenta.*
Boris Vian, *Heartsnatcher.*
Llorenç Villalonga, *The Dolls' Room.*
Toomas Vint, *An Unending Landscape.*
Ornela Vorpsi, *The Country Where No One Ever Dies.*
Austryn Wainhouse, *Hedyphagetica.*
Curtis White, *America's Magic Mountain.*
The Idea of Home.
Memories of My Father Watching TV.
Requiem.
Diane Williams, *Excitability: Selected Stories.*
Romancer Erector.
Douglas Woolf, *Wall to Wall.*
Ya! & John-Juan.
Jay Wright, *Polynomials and Pollen.*
The Presentable Art of Reading Absence.
Philip Wylie, *Generation of Vipers.*
Marguerite Young, *Angel in the Forest.*
Miss MacIntosh, My Darling.
Reyoung, *Unbabbling.*
Vlado Žabot, *The Succubus.*
Zoran Živković, *Hidden Camera.*
Louis Zukofsky, *Collected Fiction.*
Vitomil Zupan, *Minuet for Guitar.*
Scott Zwiren, *God Head.*

Swiss Literature Series

In 2008, Pro Helvetia, the Swiss Arts Council, began working with Dalkey Archive Press to identify some of the greatest and most innovative authors in twentieth and twenty-first century Swiss letters, in the tradition of such world-renowned writers as Max Frisch, Robert Walser, and Robert Pinget. Dalkey Archive editors met with critics and scholars in Zurich, Geneva, Basel, and Bern, and went on to prepare reports on numerous important Swiss authors whose work was deemed underrepresented in English. Developing from this ongoing collaboration, the Swiss Literature Series, launched in 2011 with Gerhard Meier's *Isle of the Dead* and Aglaja Veteranyi's *Why the Child Is Cooking in the Polenta*, will begin remedying this dearth of Swiss writing in the Anglophone world with a bold initiative to publish four titles a year, each supplemented with marketing efforts far exceeding what publishers can normally provide for works in translation.

With works originating from German, French, Italian, and Rhaeto-Romanic, the Swiss Literature Series will stand as a testimony to Switzerland's contribution to world literature.